SUPERNOVA

SUPERNOVA

by

DIANE ANTHONY

SUPERNOVA

Copyright © 2017 by Diane Anthony

World Ahead Press is a division of WND Books. The views and opinions expressed in this book are those of the author and do not necessarily reflect the official policy or position or WND Books.

Paperback ISBN: 978-1-944212-86-5
eBook ISBN: 978-1-944212-87-2

Printed in the United States of America
16 17 18 19 20 21 LSI 9 8 7 6 5 4 3 2 1

CONTENTS

ACKNOWLEDGEMENTS

First and foremost, to God be the glory!

I would like to thank my husband, Sage, for being here for me through it all, the good and the bad. Without your support, I never would have gotten to where I am now.

A big thank you to my best friend, Lydia, for reading my story multiple times and giving me amazing advice through it all. You are the best!

Thank you to my parents, George and Ann, for supporting me and helping me to accomplish this life goal. I love you.

To all my other friends and family who read my story and believed in me, thank you!

CHAPTER ONE

MADELINE

Dirt. That is the first thing my senses pick up, the smell of dirt, then the feel of dried grass poking into my skin. I'm lying on the ground, but I have no idea why or how I got here. I try to open my eyes, but the brightness of the summer sun causes searing pain. I push myself to a sitting position and slowly try again, allowing my eyes to adjust to the glare of the sun.

I look around and realize I'm right outside of my duplex. Gradually, I start to remember the panic. At least I think I was feeling panic. Everything seems so fuzzy. Why am I lying in the grass? Clearly, I wasn't trying to sunbathe. I'm fully dressed and I don't ever sunbathe. I'm one of those people who never achieves the highly sought after golden tan. My skin only burns. With my coppery red hair and a light complexion, well, let's just say, sunscreen is my friend. I guess I can be glad that I was lying in the shade of my maple tree. My skin might resemble the color of a cooked lobster right now.

I decide to check on Mrs. Donaldson, my recently widowed duplex neighbor. I have gotten to know her quite well since moving in about two years ago. She's such a sweet old lady. I think of her as another grandmother. A grandmother who bakes me delicious cookies . . . often. Perhaps that's why I'm not as thin as I would like to be. Oh well. I'm not going to turn down some sweet, old lady's cookies. There's not a lot Mrs. Donaldson can do to repay me for the help I give her. Arthritis is an extremely painful, terrible thing, and she's riddled with it.

I stand up and walk to her sidewalk, stumbling a bit as my head swims from the change in position. The sun-scorched grass crunches loudly under my shoes. I knock on her front door, being careful not to leave marks on the decorative glass window that I will have to clean later. I brush the dirt and grass off, trying to make myself more presentable. Perhaps, I should have gone home and checked myself in the mirror first. Too late now.

She's not answering so I knock again. I peek through the window, but I don't see her. I can't hear her coming to answer the door either. I give the door handle a try. Thoughts of her having fallen and hurting herself, or God forbid, her having passed away, run through my mind. The door is unlocked so I push the door open a crack, causing the hinges to protest with a creak. "Mrs. Donaldson? Mrs. Donaldson? It's me, Madeline." No answer. Now I'm worried. I let myself in.

I walk through her hallway, a corridor of wood flooring and light blue walls heavily decorated with pictures of her family in mismatched frames. She has three children and twelve grandchildren. Their smiling faces all look so happy. There are wedding pictures, baby pictures, school pictures, and family pictures. Pictures, pictures, pictures. It's too bad they all live in different states across the country. She gets so lonely sometimes. Her pictures are the only way she can see them on a regular basis.

I step into the living room, thinking that maybe she has fallen asleep in her wooden rocking chair again. Nope, she's not there.

"Mrs. Donaldson? It's me, Madeline. Sorry to barge in on you. Your door was open and I just wanted to check on you."

I hear a small murmur from the kitchen. I make my way back to the hallway and toward the sound. I see the bottom of her slippered feet first and realize that she's lying on the hard linoleum floor. I run into the room, calling out frantically, "Mrs. Donaldson! Mrs. Donaldson!"

She grunts again and twitches her hand. I kneel next to her and shake her gently. I carefully lift her head onto my lap. Her eyelids flutter a little, exposing her pale blue eyes momentarily. "Mrs. Donaldson! Are you okay?" She starts coming to.

"Madeline, dear? Why am I on the floor?" She asks, looking around wide eyed. Her voice cracks from disuse.

"I was going to ask you the same thing. This is so weird. I just woke up outside, lying in the grass, and I don't have any idea how I got there. What's going on?" I ask more to myself, than to her.

I help Mrs. Donaldson up to one of the padded chairs by the kitchen table. Her frail frame is shaking as she moves.

"Here. Have a seat. I'll get you some water."

I open the oak cupboard door next to the sink and get out two tall glasses. I realize I'm feeling parched as well. How long was I lying outside? I see about four dozen chocolate chip cookies on the counter. Mrs. Donaldson was baking again. I smile at the thought of how much joy baking brings her. She always hums to herself when she bakes, with a sparkle in her eye. I grab a small china plate out of another cupboard and bring some cookies to the table.

"How do you feel, Mrs. Donaldson?"

I set a glass of water in front of her and the plate between us.

"I'm feeling all right, dear. A little sore and a bit tingly all over, but otherwise I think I'm fine. I can't for the life of me figure out why I would be on the floor, though," She says, her voice fading away with a tremble.

She takes a small sip of water, the glass shaking as she lifts it to her mouth. I grab a cookie off the plate and take a bite. It's crumbly and stale. Mrs. Donaldson's cookies are always so soft and delicious. She never makes mistakes. She has years of practice.

"Hmm. These cookies seem to have been sitting out for a while. When did you make them?" I ask, setting the cookie back down hoping she won't be offended.

"I woke up early, as usual, and got some chores done. Then after eating lunch, I decided to bake some cookies. I had just taken the last pan out of the oven, but . . . I don't remember anything after that. I don't know how long I've been lying on the floor. I always have aches and pains, so it's hard to tell from that."

"I'm sorry. Would you like me to get your pain medications?"

"Not yet, dear. I still feel a bit off. Do you know what time it is?"

I look past her at the clock on the stove, but it's blank. The wall clock I gave her for Christmas last year, one of those clocks where a different bird sings its song every top of the hour, seems to have stopped too. I stand up and try to turn on a light. Nothing.

"The power seems to be out. Let me check my cell phone," I say, reaching into my front pants pocket. I pull my phone out and press the power button. Nothing. I just charged it this morning. Weird.

"My cell phone battery is dead. I'll see if I can figure out the time and get back to you. Are you going to be all right, Mrs. Donaldson? Is there anything else I can get for you before I go?"

"I'll be fine. Thank you, Madeline. Go take care of those precious cats of yours. Who knows how long we've been out. The poor dears might be starving," she says with a stronger voice. At least she seems to be calming down a bit.

I feel bad leaving Mrs. Donaldson alone with all this confusion, but I'll come back to check on her once I figure some things out. I give her hand a reassuring squeeze.

"I'll be back in a little while."

She gives my hand a light squeeze in return. As I head over to my side of the duplex, I look at the building next to ours and consider checking in on Ian; he's my gorgeous neighbor. I take a couple of steps in his direction, but stop. I have no idea what I would say to him. I decide it would be super awkward so I just turn around and go home. As soon as I open my door, I'm greeted with a frenzy of meows and leg rubbings. My poor cats seem desperate for food, but then again, that always seems to be the case as soon as their dishes are empty.

I walk to my kitchen at the end of the hallway, and find that their food dishes are not only licked clean, but have been slid all the way across the floor. I scoot the dishes back into place and fill them with food and water. I pet my babies for a short while. Midnight, my black cat, purrs and continues to come to me for some ear scratching in between her mouthfuls of food. Euphrates, my male calico cat, who is always so lovey, just eats. He must have been starving.

I stand up and stretch out some of my stiff muscles. The effort makes me realize just how stifling it is in my duplex, now that the air conditioner isn't working. How did people manage to live like this before air conditioners were invented? I open some windows hoping maybe that will cool things off; unlikely, since it's just about as hot outside. I should call my parents and see how they're doing. Since they don't live in town, maybe they still have electricity and will let me stay with them if mine doesn't come back on soon.

I go to the storage closet that's next to the bathroom and start searching for my old, corded phone. I am greeted with stuff, upon stuff, upon stuff: extra blankets, extension cords, board games, a box of my high school memorabilia my mom didn't feel like keeping at her house anymore, instruction manuals for every appliance and electronic device I own, old sweatshirts, rain gear, even a slightly used tarp my dad gave me for camping. I should really get rid of some of it. How could I have possibly acquired this much junk already? Aha! There it is, under my sleeping bag and the tennis racket I got for my birthday last year. Clearly, I haven't even used it since it still has the label on the head of the racket.

I walk back to the kitchen and unplug the cordless phone from the phone jack so I can plug in my corded one. I pick up the handset and think for a second about what my mom's number is. Call lists on cell phones are a blessing and a curse all at the same time. I finish dialing and wait. I know how our conversation is inevitably going to go. "You should go out on a date with so and so. He's such a nice boy. You need to settle down like Elizabeth. That girl has her head on straight." Blah, blah, blah.

Don't get me wrong, my mom, well, both of my parents, have my best interests in mind. They care deeply for my brother and me, sometimes annoyingly so. Yes, Elizabeth, who happens to be my best friend in the whole world, chose to get married at a young age . . . right out of high school to be exact. But I'm not in any hurry to get married. I know that I will find a guy sometime, but I'm not too worried about that right now.

The phone has rung three times now which isn't like her. She usually picks up after two rings. Just as I'm about to worry, she finally answers.

"Hello?"

"Mom!"

"Hello, Goose!"

That has been my mom's nickname for me since I was around six years old. It has something to do with me trying to feed a goose some bread while on vacation at the lake. The goose charged me. I dropped the bread and ran, screaming my head off with the crazy bird chasing after me. It bit my butt and caused serious psychological damage, I swear. I can't hear a goose honking in the sky without my heart rate jumping and having a sudden urge to cover my backside. My mom thought it was the funniest thing ever.

"Hey, do you have power over at your house?"

"No, we don't. Your father and I just woke up a little while ago. We must have fallen asleep on the couch while watching the television. It's odd, though. We're not usually nappers."

"This is getting weird! I just woke up outside in my front lawn. I have no idea why or how long I was out there. I went over to check on Mrs. Donaldson and she was passed out on the floor. She's fine, but I'm starting to freak out a little."

"Have you given your brother a call?" she asks, with an edge of panic in her voice.

"Nope. Matthew is probably at the lab anyway," I say, rolling my eyes. "You're the first one I called."

Matthew is my *genius* brother. He's in his last year of college for cell and molecular biology. He's the top of his class, just like in high school. I think he could have gotten into a school for gifted people back then, but he chose to stay where he was so he could keep his friends. I wish he would have left though. Every teacher I had after him expected me to be as smart and gifted as he was, and every single teacher was disappointed when they found out I was just an average student. Matthew liked to pretend to be normal back then, but now that he is in college, normalcy has been thrown out the window, along with his chance of ever getting a girlfriend. I swear he eats, sleeps, and practically lives in the lab. Nerd.

"I'm glad you called to let us know you're okay. I think I'll try to give Matthew a call. Make sure you eat something. Who knows how long it's been since you last ate."

I am twenty-three years old. Technically, I have been an adult for five years, living on my own, completing college, and paying bills like any other responsible adult . . . and yet my mother still worries that I don't know how to take care of myself.

"Okay, Mom. Once I'm off the phone, I'll find something to snack on. I'm glad you and Dad are all right. I'm going to give Elizabeth a call and see if she knows anything more. If I find anything out, I'll give you a call."

"Please do, Goose. Love you!" my mom says, her voice still tense.

"Love you too, Mom. Tell Dad I love him too. Bye."

After I hang up the phone, a thought pops in my head: If my parents, Mrs. Donaldson, and I all fell asleep, did other people fall asleep too? And what could those people have been doing when they fell sleep? What if some were driving? Or swimming in the lake? Or flying in an airplane?

Maybe I'm overreacting. Maybe it was just some sort of freak coincidence that we all fell asleep at the same time. I take a deep calming breath. It doesn't do any good to sit around worrying. I'll see if Elizabeth's okay after I grab something to eat.

I head to my refrigerator. The power is out, so I'll need to be quick. Before I open the door, I decide to grab an apple. I swing the door open and a rank smell hits my nose. My milk has definitely gone bad. I thought I had a couple of days before it expired. Guess not. I cover my nose with my shirt and grab an apple out of the fruit drawer. Everything in here seems to be room temperature. How long has the power been out? I'm going to have to pitch a lot of my food. Sad. Payday doesn't come until . . . until when? I still don't know what day it is.

Uh-oh! The last time I remember, it was Sunday! Should I be at work?

I'm a librarian at the public library. It's one of my favorite places here in town, tied for first with King Cone, the ice cream shop. Probably another reason I've got a few extra pounds.

Amherst is a typical small, Wisconsin town. There are at least as many bars as there are churches. An antiques store, a couple of mom and pop diners, and a few other businesses that apparently get enough customers to stay open. Overall, it's not a bad place to live.

I eat my apple and then start to call Elizabeth. Wait . . . does Elizabeth have a corded phone? She's smart. I'm sure she has one.

"Hello?"

It's Philip. Her husband.

"Hello, Philip. Is Elizabeth there?"

"Yeah. Just a second."

I hear him put his hand over the phone and call out for Elizabeth.

"You can talk to her, but don't take forever."

Yup. Philip is kind of a jerk to me.

"Hello?"

I hear Philip give her a kiss on the cheek. He loves her deeply, but me? Not so much. If I had to guess, I think he may be jealous of our friendship. We have a kind of bond that he will never have with her. Twenty years of friendship is nothing to scoff at.

"Hey, Elizabeth."

"Madeline! Oh my God! Do you know what time it is? We just woke up in our car. Thank God we were in our driveway and not driving down the road when we fell asleep. But now our car won't work. Seems like our battery died and our power is out, too," she spills out, frantically.

Shoot! They fell asleep too. Looks like it must be more than just a coincidence.

"Wow! I'm glad you guys are okay. And no, I don't know what time it is. That's why I called you. Things are so messed up. I'm not even sure what day it is or whether I'm supposed to be at work or not."

"I don't know what day it is either," she says, pausing a moment while she thinks about it. "I can't imagine you would have a lot of people showing up in a blackout, though. And I'm guessing it would be difficult to keep track of people checking books in and out without the computer, let alone without lights to be able to see the books."

"You're right, I guess. Maybe I'll head down there and check on things in a little while. I wish someone knew what time it was."

"Me too. I'm kind of freaking out!"

I can hear Philip in the background, "Elizabeth, you should finish this up. Someone else might be trying to call us."

And by someone else, I know he really means someone more important.

"I should probably go, Madeline. If you find anything out, please call me."

"Absolutely, I will. Stay safe."

Man, I miss my friend. At least, how our friendship used to be: going to movies, bowling, just hanging out and talking for hours. I'm so lost in thought, I nearly fall off the kitchen chair when I hear pounding on my front door. As I get up to go answer it, they pound again.

"Coming," I call out.

Knock! Knock! Knock!

Sheesh! This person is persistent. I open the door and there stands Matthew. He's got blood covering half of his face.

CHAPTER TWO

VINCENT

"**G**ood God! What is that smell?" Vincent asks himself, waking to the stench of stale urine and mildew. He opens his eyes to find that he is lying on the hard, concrete floor of his jail cell. His face is just a few inches away from the toilet. He scrambles to sit up and put as much distance as he can away from the disgusting floor. As soon as he's sitting on his bed, he realizes that his head and right shoulder are throbbing with pain.

How long was I laying on the floor? Sick!

He massages his muscular shoulder, trying to get the pain to stop. He lifts his hand to his forehead near his right temple and touches it gingerly. He flinches as a sharp pain passes into his skull. His finger touches something crusty on his head. He gently scratches a bit off and sees dried blood under his fingernails. He looks down at the floor where he woke up and there's a small puddle of blood where he was lying.

What the hell?

He gets up from the bed and studies a dark spot on the toilet seat. The sun filtering in from his small barred window shines on the blackish-maroon stain.

That looks like blood too. What the hell is going on? I can't remember anything. I musta hit my head on the toilet before goin' unconscious on the floor. But why?

He looks at himself in the small plastic mirror above the sink to assess the damage. The cut is right along his hair line. The blood almost blends in with his short dark brown hair. He wonders for a moment how hard he hit his head. He's had a few concussions in his day from getting in fights, so he is familiar with some of the warning signs. His pupils appear to be the same size, and since he doesn't have a flashlight, he will just have to assume he's fine. He takes a closer look at his reflection. He has bags under his chestnut eyes and scruffy facial hair surrounding his meticulously groomed goatee.

How long was I laying there?

He tries to search for any memory of what could have happened. He starts to pace his cell like he always does when he's worked up. He can walk all of four steps before turning around to do it again. His hard-soled shoes make a clacking noise as he walks on the solid concrete. It suddenly hits him just how quiet the jail is. He decides to ask his buddy Frank if maybe he knows what happened to him.

It's the middle of the day, there should be more noise than this, he thinks as the silence starts to feel heavy in his ears.

He peers across the hall to Frank's cell. Frank is lying at an odd angle on his bed. It looks as though he sat on the edge of the bed, tipped over sideways, and fell asleep with his feet still touching the floor.

"Frank," Vincent whispers. "Frank, can you hear me?"

Frank lays still. Vincent grabs hold of his cell bars to try to get a good look in the hallway. He sees Officer Williams laying in a heap on the floor four cells away. *What's going on? Did someone hit the prison with knockout gas or what?* He turns his head and presses his face against the bars to look down the hall the other way. The cell door creaks open.

What the . . .

He pushes the door open just enough to get out and then hesitates, waiting for a guard to start shouting at him. Nothing. He cautiously steps out of the cell.

"Frank," he calls out louder. "Yo, Frank!"

Frank twitches. Vincent can hear him intake a sharp breath and then he sits up, the bed protesting under his heavy weight.

Vincent steps up to Frank's cell. He grabs a hold of the cold, black bars on the cell door and pulls. His door opens too.

"How'd you do that? You're gonna get us in trouble, man!" Frank says, his long, dirty blonde hair flopping in front of his face as he leans forward to stand up.

"I don't think so," he says, pointing to the guard on the floor.

Vincent looks down the hall. The always glowing exit light is out.

"Powers out or somethin'," Vincent says.

Frank steps out of the cell, his round face scrunched up in confusion. Officer Williams starts to stir. Vincent sees his chance of freedom slipping away and rushes over to grab the guard's baton and set of keys. The sounds of bed squeaks and slight mumblings fill the jail as other prisoners start coming to.

"Let's go, man!" Frank shouts to Vincent.

They turn and run down the hall to the staircase.

"Hey! Stop right there!" Officer Williams yells, standing up. He reaches for his baton, but finds it's not there. His hand instinctively goes to the radio on his shoulder.

"We have a 10-98! I repeat a 10-98 in progress!" He says, but he notices that there is no static sound when he lets go of the talk button. He clicks the button a few times. Dead silence. He starts to chase after them.

Vincent and Frank make it to the black metal staircase and continue running down them. Another officer is trying to stand up at the base of the stairs, unaware of what is happening. He hears Williams shouting and his hand goes to his baton.

"Don't do it!" Vincent warns. He reaches him before the officer has his weapon out, and bashes him in the side of the head with the stolen baton. The officer falls to the floor, facedown. Vincent gives him another blow on the back of the skull, just to make sure.

The prison is growing louder with the shouts of the inmates, cell doors slamming open, and shoes scuffling as prisoners start making a break for it.

Officer Williams is almost down the stairs. They turn to their right and run to the end of the hallway on the main floor. Vincent looks behind him to see how close the guard is. Williams picks up the fallen guard's baton and starts after them. Just as he does, a prisoner steps out of his cell and grabs Officer Williams from behind. He puts him in a choke hold, as another inmate rips the baton out of the officer's hand and starts beating Williams with it.

"Hey, thanks!" Vincent yells to them as he comes to a locked door.

Let's hope I can find the right key, Vincent thinks, adrenaline coursing through his veins. *We just might make it!*

Vincent fumbles with the keychain, trying key after key in the lock.

"Hurry up, Vinny," Frank says nervously.

"Don't call me 'Vinny'," Vincent warns him, testily.

After trying about a dozen keys, he finally finds the right one. The metal door swings open and he continues running, with Frank puffing behind.

One more door and we're free!

He had been down this concrete hallway many times over the last eighteen months, on his way to work in the laundry room. He always dreamed about making a break for it, but of course he couldn't with all the guards around. The excitement of breaking free gives him a renewed vigor. *Focus!*

Vincent slows down at the end of the hall where it cuts off to the left and leads to the main entrance. He stops and peeks around the corner. The guard standing at the main entrance has his gun drawn and looks scared out of his mind. He's a new guy who just took the job a few weeks ago, fresh out of training. Apparently, he isn't sure what he's supposed to do. He can clearly hear the riot from where he's standing. He takes a couple of tentative steps as though he's going to go check on what's going on, but then thinks better of it and stays put.

While the guard is looking down a hallway that's facing the other way, Vincent runs as silent as he can behind the guard and slams the baton against the back of his head, just before the guard turns. The guard stumbles forward, but doesn't fall. *Damn, he's tougher than he looks.* The guard catches his footing and spins around, bringing the gun up, his hands shaking violently. Vincent hits the guard's arm hard, causing him to drop the gun. Frank picks up the gun, as Vincent knees the guard in the soft parts. The guard falls to the ground, curled up in a ball.

"Sorry," Frank mutters, as he smashes his heel against the guard's head. The guard goes still, buying Vincent time to find the right key.

"Come on, man," Frank says, panicky. He stands next to the wall, peeking around the corner, watching for someone to catch them.

"Shut up! Your nagging is makin' me forget which keys I've tried," Vincent says, trying yet another key in the lock. The cacophony of the riot echoes in his ears, making it hard to concentrate.

Finally, they make it outside. Vincent takes a deep breath of fresh air to help clear his head. They do a quick scan and don't see anyone. Together, they take off running down the driveway.

"We just gotta make it past the guard towers and we're free!" Frank says, out of breath.

Vincent makes it to the gate before Frank does. He starts the next key guessing game with the largest key on the chain. To his relief, it clicks home. He pushes the gate open, but his hope vanishes when he hears a gunshot ring out from overhead.

"Grrhh!" Frank grunts.

Vincent turns back around in time to see Frank fall to the ground with a hole blown in his left shoulder. Frank struggles to push himself up with his good arm, holding his injured arm tightly to his body. Vincent runs over to give him a hand, praying that the guard doesn't shoot him too. He picks up the gun Frank dropped when he fell and helps pull Frank up to his feet, which isn't easy, since Frank weighs at least a hundred pounds more than Vincent. He finally gets his feet under himself, and with Vincent's help, makes it to the gate just as another shot is fired. It hits the metal gate, missing them by mere inches. They throw themselves up against the wall of the tower, just out of the guard's sight.

"What are we gonna do," Frank asks, with a moan of pain.

Vincent looks around at the situation. The stone guard tower, where the guard just shot from, is one of two towers that stand at the entrance of the prison, connected by the metal entry gate. He can't spot a guard in the second tower's windows. *Let's hope it stays that way*, Vincent thinks. A solid stone wall runs around the perimeter of the facility with coiled, stainless steel barbed wire along the top. There is nothing for them to take cover behind for their escape.

"Stay here," Vincent whispers to Frank.

He keeps his back pressed up against the tower wall and edges his way to the door. He starts trying keys in the lock as silently as he can. Frank is leaning against the wall, breathing heavy, his face looking pale, and his shirt soaked in blood.

"Why hasn't the guard come down here and finished us off yet?" Frank asks quietly, panting.

"He knows all he's gotta do is stand there and wait. There's nowhere for us to go. As soon as we step away from this wall, we're dead," Vincent whispers.

Frank closes his eyes and swallows hard, shaking.

After trying what feels like the entire key chain, Vincent finds the right key. He pulls the door open, and sees a metal stairway leading up to the guard. He grabs the handrail and starts his ascent as slowly and quietly as his shaking muscles will allow. He slows his breathing, trying to calm his nerves.

If he ever wants to see his little girl again, he knows he's going to have to do this.

He keeps his eyes trained upward as he climbs the stairs. Once he gets closer to the top, he can make out the guard standing at the ready, with his rifle aimed toward the ground, where Frank is standing just out of sight. Vincent takes two more steps up and aims his gun at the guard's head, finger on the trigger. He takes a deep breath, trying to control the shaking in his hands and squeezes the trigger. The guard crumples to the ground, blood pooling on the floor around him.

Vincent lowers the gun, heart pounding and ears ringing. He makes it down the stairs, taking two at a time. He pushes the door open and runs back to Frank, who is now sitting on the ground, holding pressure on the wound.

"Come on, we gotta get outta here," Vincent says, hooking his arm under Frank's good one. He strains, as he tries to help him up off the ground. "You gotta stand up, Frank. We gotta go!"

He looks back at the prison entrance and sees prisoners spilling out of the doorway.

"Crap! We gotta go now!" Vincent shouts.

Frank gets himself off the ground and they start trotting away from the prison.

CHAPTER THREE

MADELINE

"Oh my goodness! Matthew!" I grab his arm and wrap it around my shoulder. He accepts the help and leans his weight onto me. I have him sit down in my recliner and run to the kitchen to get a wet towel so I can clean him up.

I start scrubbing off the blood. It's all dried and crusted on his face. There's also a big blood stain on his right leg. The laceration is just below the shaggy black hair on his forehead. I have no medical background, but it doesn't look like he will need stitches.

"What happened? Are you all right?"

"Yeah. I think so, but my head hurts, and my whole body tingles. I think I'm dehydrated. Could I have a glass of water, please?"

I hand him the towel and go get him some water. I slip into the bathroom to grab some pain killers from my medicine cabinet. As I reach for the bottle, I almost knock it over. My hands are shaking so bad.

I head back to the living room. "Here. I brought you some pain killers, too. Tell me what happened!"

I wait while he pops the tablets in his mouth and swallows them with the whole glass of water.

"I finished with some work I was doing in the lab and decided to visit you to return the movies you let me borrow. I was about half a mile away from your place and . . . and . . . that's all I can remember. I woke up in my car, my head against the steering wheel, blood was all over the place, and my head was throbbing horribly. My car was in the ditch, so that must explain why I was injured, but I don't remember what happened. And to top it all off, my car won't start. It won't even turn over!" he pauses for a moment, closing his eyes and pinching the bridge of his nose. "What day is today?"

"I have no idea. I woke up in my front lawn this morning. Everyone I've talked to doesn't know what happened or what day it is, either, and the power is out. If you drove into a ditch, then other people must have too. Did you happen to see any other cars when you walked here?"

"Not that I can remember. I was only about half a mile away from your house."

"Man, I wish I could watch the news right now to see what's going on!" Nervously, I start picking at the skin around my nails, a bad habit I started when I was a child.

Matthew stands up and gives me a reassuring hug. "Mads, it is going to be okay. There must be a logical explanation for all of this. We'll figure it out." He looks down at his blood-stained pants. "Do you have some spare clothes I could borrow?"

I dress a bit like a tom boy, almost always wearing jeans and t-shirts when I'm not at work.

"I don't think my jeans will fit you, but I have some sweatpants and a shirt you can wear." I go to my bedroom and grab him some clothes. Matthew is taller and thinner than me, but they will have to do for now.

After he changes, we sit in my living room to talk. Midnight jumps on my lap for some snuggles, and Euphrates noses his way onto Matthew's lap.

"Have you heard from Mom and Dad?" asks Matthew.

"I called them. She said she was going to call you. Does your cell phone work?"

"No. Once I woke up in my car and realized my car wouldn't start, I tried to call you to have you come get me, but my phone wouldn't turn on."

"My phone wouldn't turn on either, even though I had just charged it. Mom said they had just woke up on the couch. As a matter of fact, everyone I've talked to so far has said that they just woke up," I pause, thinking. "So, let's see, the power is out, cars won't start, cell phone batteries are dead, and everyone just spontaneously falls asleep for some undetermined amount of time. I hope we start figuring out what's going on soon."

"Me too," he says. "Hey, are you okay with me staying here while we try to find some answers?"

"No problem. You can take the spare bedroom. I'll just have to tidy it up a bit. Before I go do that, are you hungry? It smells like some of my food has gone bad in the fridge, but I think I can manage to throw something together."

After a supper of spam and baked beans, Matthew and I decide to take a walk down to the fire department and see if they have any information. As we walk through town, we notice small groups of people gathered together in front lawns, talking.

"Did you want to stop and talk to them? See if they know more information?" Matthew offers.

I sort of do, but I don't like interjecting myself into other people's conversations. I'm not sure what I would say, either. Just thinking about walking up to them makes me feel nervous.

"Nah. Let's just head to the fire department. If anyone has any answers, I would think it would be them."

As we get closer to the fire department, we see that there is already a large crowd standing around a few firemen. We can hear people in the crowd all trying to ask questions at the same time. We stay to the back and listen.

"What about my electricity? I can't go to bed until after I've watched the evening news!" an old man demands.

"Sir, the electricians will do whatever they can to get things up and running in this town. You need to be patient," says one of the firemen.

"I saw some hooligans breaking into the grocery store and stealing food! Where are the police?" a middle-aged woman asks, outraged.

"Ma'am, the police are dealing with a lot right now. There have been a lot of accidents reported…"

"Reported? How? My phone doesn't work!" she interrupts.

"With a corded phone, duh!" pipes in a teenaged boy.

"Don't you sass me, young man!" She yells.

"People! People! Just calm down. I know it's scary not knowing what's going on. We're doing our best to figure things out. We all need to just remain calm, and stick together. If you find anything out, please report it and we'll make sure everyone knows what's going on."

"Looks like there aren't any answers yet. Want to head back?" I ask Matthew quietly.

"Sure," Matthew agrees.

We get back to my duplex just as it's getting dark.

"I'm not sure if I will actually fall asleep, but I'm going to bed. My head is starting to ache again," Matthew yawns. "Night, Mads."

I stay up a little while longer, sitting in my brown, well-worn, hand me down recliner, with cats on my lap, warm and purring. I take the time to thank God that Matthew is still alive, as well as everyone else that I care about. I rest my head back and start to doze off.

It is an overcast, gray day. I'm standing in my front lawn, when suddenly I hear a low rumbling sound, a sound that I feel vibrating in my very bones. I look up to the sky and there is a brilliant blue flash that permeates everything around me. I hear a neighbor screaming as I fall backwards and black out.

I startle awake. I'm covered in a cold sweat, my heart is racing out of my chest, and my breathing is rapid, like I just ran a mile. After I calm myself down a bit, I decide to make my way to my bedroom to sleep. I groggily force myself to change into my pajamas and brush my teeth before crawling into bed. Just before I fall asleep, the thought creeps in my mind, *what if that wasn't a dream but a memory?*

CHAPTER FOUR

VINCENT

"Give me your phone. I gotta make a call!" Vincent demands, waking up his buddy, Pete.

"My cell ain't workin'" Pete answers, groggily.

"Neither's mine. Where's Frank's phone?" he asks, getting agitated.

"I don't know. Where he left it before you guys got thrown in the slammer. Told you not to rob that store . . . " Pete responds, turning his long lanky body to face the back of the ratty couch in hopes of falling asleep again. He keeps his knees bent with his feet hanging off the cushion in order to fit on the couch.

Vincent walks into the next room where Frank is sleeping. Pete stayed up all night trying to fix Frank's shoulder. He was able to dig the bullet out and stitch him up, but there's no telling if he's going to make it or not. His doctoring skills are rudimentary, at best. Frank lost consciousness after they poured whiskey on his shoulder to sterilize the wound and hasn't woken up since. He lost a lot of blood.

Vincent moves quietly next to the bed. There is nothing but a lamp and a gun sitting on top of the water stained, rickety nightstand. He opens the drawer and finds another gun and some loose ammunition. No cell phone. He turns around and walks across the dirty brown, shag carpet to the dresser. He opens every drawer and only finds more guns, more ammunition, and some spare clothes.

He must have had his phone on him when he was thrown in jail. It's gone now.

He walks back out of the room and heads towards the kitchen. Stale crumbs crunch under his shoes as he makes his way to the cordless phone sitting on the cluttered counter next to the rusty fridge. He picks up the handset. Dead. He slams it back in the charger, knocking a pile of newspapers onto the floor. Anger swelling, he picks up an empty beer bottle and throws it against the wall, shattering it into pieces.

"What the hell was that?" Pete calls out.

"I need a phone!" Vincent growls.

"Why?"

"I need to check up on my little girl."

"Go ask the neighbors," Pete suggests angrily.

Their hideout is in an old, rundown apartment building. They only have a few neighbors that still live here. Most of them are drug addicts, almost continuously using. It was a good place for Vincent and his friends to meet and plan their jobs. Nobody around there bothered to ask any questions. The one downfall of the location is the foul-smelling fog of smoke always hanging in the building, seeping into their own apartment. It makes it perpetually hazy and hard to breathe at times.

Vincent opens the front door, pulling hard to get it unstuck. He knocks on the door directly across the hall. Nobody answers.

"Hey. I need to use your phone." Vincent calls out.

Again, no answer. He knocks once more and puts his ear against the door. He can't hear anything. He turns the doorknob and finds that the door is unlocked. He pushes the door open and a rancid stench hits him. He gags, almost losing his breakfast. *What the . . . ?* He coughs and covers his nose with his shirt. He glances around, trying to spot the source and sees his middle-aged neighbor slumped on the couch, dead. A tourniquet is still wrapped tightly around his skinny upper arm with a heroin needle sticking out of his inner elbow. His white cloudy eyes are wide open, staring up toward the crumbling ceiling.

Poor bastard.

Vincent averts his eyes, disgusted. He starts searching for a corded phone. He walks through the dingy living room, giving the dead man a wide berth. He steps into the kitchen and finds a phone hanging on the wall by a fold-up card table the guy must have used to eat on. The table is covered with crumbs and a white powdery substance running in faint lines. *How many drugs was this guy on?*

He unplugs the phone to take it back to his place, not wanting to spend one more second in this dump than he must. Once he has the phone in his hands, he quickens his pace to leave, and closes the door tightly behind him. He takes a deep breath, finally able to breathe again. *God, I hope this stench washes off,* he thinks, taking a sniff at his shirt.

He heads to his kitchen, where the only phone jack in the apartment is located, and plugs in the phone. He dials his ex's number.

"Hello?" answers a weak voice.

"Stacy, it's Vincent."

"Vinny? How you callin' me? Ain't you in jail?" Stacy asks, sniffling.

"My cell door was unlocked and everyone was asleep or somethin', so me and Frankie made a break for it. Frankie got shot in the shoulder. He'll live, I think."

Stacy starts to cry.

"What? What's goin' on?"

"It's Maggie…"

"What's wrong with Maggie? Where's she at?"

"Oh God, Vinny! I don't know how it happened! One minute she's takin' a bath and I'm sittin' in the bathroom with her, readin' a magazine and the next minute, I wake up lyin' on the bathroom floor and Maggie was face down in the water," Stacy says through sobs.

"What?!"

"I-I-I p-picked her up outta the water and sh-sh-she wasn't breathin'. Oh God!" Stacy pauses, unable to speak through her crying.

"Did you call an ambulance? Give her mouth to mouth? What the hell did you do to save my little girl!?" Vincent screams.

"I…I was gonna call 911, but my cell phone didn't work. I was in shock, Vinny. I wasn't thinkin' clearly. Her body . . . it . . . it looked wrong. I don't know how long I was sleepin' but she was cold as ice, and . . . bloated . . . " she stops talking, and Vincent can hear her throwing up in the background.

Vincent slams the phone down, hanging up on Stacy. He flops down on the ripped-up vinyl kitchen chair, staring numbly at nothing in particular. *My baby! Why!?* Every muscle in his body starts to go rigid. He balls his hands into fists and before he knows what he's doing, he's up on his feet tearing apart the kitchen. He punches the wall, making a gaping hole in the dry wall.

"What the hell is your problem?!" Pete yells from the couch.

Vincent grabs the table and sends it flying across the room, knocking into the cabinets, and throws his chair, nearly missing Pete who's now standing in the doorway watching his friend lose it.

"She's dead!" Vincent screams in Pete's direction. He lets out a gut-wrenching yell, until his face turns red and his throat goes raw. He falls to the floor and starts weeping, ripping at his hair.

"Oh man," Pete's face softens. "I'm sorry." He places a hand on his shoulder, then leaves the room for Vincent to grieve in peace.

CHAPTER FIVE

MADELINE

A week has past and life is starting to come back to Amherst. Some parts of town have electricity. Unfortunately, that's not my side of town, but at least the library has power. I see tow trucks driving around retrieving cars to take to the shop and fix. Utility trucks are all over town with electricians working like mad to get the electricity back up and running.

Matthew and I have been taking turns riding my bike to the local high school, which is about a mile away from my place, whenever we need to use the facilities or take showers. The school has power back on and has kindly opened the gymnasium to those who do not have their electricity yet. I took my power cord along with me to charge my cell phone. I can finally turn it on, but there is still no service.

Constant bike rides are a pain, but it's good for me, works off some of those cookies from Mrs. Donaldson. She has a friend she's been staying with in the part of town that has electricity. I hope things return to normal soon. Man, I miss her cookies.

I'm in the kitchen, scrounging up what I can find for breakfast, when Matthew comes in.

"Good news, Mads! I just got off the phone with the car shop. They said they will get my car in today. I'll be out of your hair soon."

"Good! Not the part about you being out of my hair . . . good that they can get your car in," I say, which is partly true.

"Thanks for letting me stay here for the last week. It was a nice break from school, but it's time for me to get back there and see if anyone knows more about what's going on and how I can help."

"I'm just glad Professor McGreggor was so understanding about everything."

Matthew had called Professor McGreggor, one of his teachers at the university, to explain what is going on. I can tell he is fond of Matthew. But then again, *genius* Matthew is one of the brightest in his class and charming, to boot. Who doesn't love him? Everything he does is perfect. Even when we were children, he hardly ever got into trouble. It was always me screwing up and getting grounded. Although, some of the choices I made were despite my brother. Matthew prided himself on his school attendance record and refused to ever skip a day of school unless he was deathly ill because he believed it was "irresponsible and dishonest". So, when Elizabeth would ask me to skip out on school to hang out at the beach for a day, I couldn't resist. Eventually, my parents would find out and I would get in trouble, but the look of disapproval on Matthew's face always made the lectures about being "more like your brother" worth it. I know my parents love me, but I can tell that they're prouder of Matthew and everything he has accomplished, even if they try to hide it from me.

When he had called the professor, Matthew happened to be standing in the kitchen with me. He suddenly got excited and said, "Wait just a moment, Professor. My sister needs to hear this."

He took the phone away from his ear and whispered, "He just said he knows how long we were all blacked out!"

Matthew put his phone on speaker. "Okay, Professor, please start from the beginning."

"Well, as I was saying, Matthew, I had just made some bacterial cultures in the lab and was on my way home, when the phenomenon happened. After I woke up, and no one seemed to know how long we were unconscious or what time it was, I remembered the cultures. I walked back to the lab and was able to discern by the growth of the bacteria about how long we were unconscious," he said, then paused.

"And!?" I blurted out before I could stop myself. The suspense was killing me.

"And, the culture showed two days' worth of growth."

Matthew and I were stunned. Two whole days?

"Thank you, Professor," I said.

After Matthew finished his conversation, I called Mom and Elizabeth with the update.

Matthew and I took a walk down to the fire department to share what we had just heard. They contacted the newspaper and within twenty-four hours, I spotted people standing in their yards with a paper in their hands, gossiping about it. Word travels fast around here.

That was four days ago.

Matthew and I sit down to a hearty breakfast of buttered bread and the last of my apples. I feel like I have been camping for the past week, only using disposable dinnerware and coolers with ice. Oh well. I like camping.

After breakfast, he helps me clean up a bit and then heads down to AJ's Service Station to see how the repairs are going. To be honest, I'm glad he'll be heading home soon. I love my brother, but he has been getting on my nerves this last week. He kept trying to "help" me by telling me how to do things in my own house. That's how he's always been though. He has systems for doing every menial task imaginable. Most of the time I refused to change things, even though his way usually was more efficient.

You know, if you put the bottles of water in the cooler first and then add the ice, you will fit more in the cooler at a time.

You should leave the pan off the burner when lighting it so you can avoid the flare up once the gas ignites.

Look, if you squeeze the toothpaste from the bottom and work your way up instead of squeezing it in the middle, you can save yourself a lot of time later and get the most out of the tube.

I'm definitely looking forward to things being back to normal.

I sit down to read a library book I brought home yesterday. Mrs. Yates, the other librarian I work with, decided that we would switch off and work every other day until things are back to normal. She has power in her house, but she said that TV stations are not up yet. That leads us to believe whatever happened, happened everywhere.

I'm just getting into my story when I hear the hum of my refrigerator. Yes! My electricity is back on! You never realize just how much ambient noise there is until all your appliances and electronics no longer work. Just out of curiosity, I walk over to my TV and turn it on. Still no stations.

I call Mrs. Donaldson's friend to let them know that our electricity is working and that Mrs. Donaldson can return home. After I'm off the phone, I go outside for a bit to enjoy this beautiful day. As I'm sitting in my lawn chair reading, Matthew drives up in his car.

"Well, I'm on my way!" he says, getting out of his car. "Thanks again for putting up with me for the last week."

"That's what family is for. Oh, guess what? My power is back on!"

"You are one strange girl, sis."

"What?"

"Your power is finally back on and you come outside instead of enjoying it," Matthew teases.

I give him a playful punch on the arm.

"Ow! Watch the guns, Mads," he responds with mock pain.

He gives me a quick, awkward one-armed hug and turns to leave. He's never been good at saying goodbye.

Once he's in his car, he rolls down the window, "I'll give you a call as soon I as I find anything out."

"Same thing for me, too."

I stand, waving until he's out of sight. I sigh and start walking to go back inside, remembering that the laundry has been building up for far too long. Time to get to work. Just as I'm almost to my door, I hear the neighbor boys across the road laughing. They are tossing a football down the sidewalk to each other while their mother is over at the neighbor's house having a deep conversation, not really paying attention. It's four-year-old Jimmy, tossing the football to his six-year-old brother, Thomas, who happens to be a couple of houses away. I stop to wave to them.

"Wow! Good arm!" I say to myself. Strange. I'm not an expert on children, but two houses seems to be a remarkable distance for a four-year-old. I'm not even sure I could throw a football that far. I just shrug my shoulders and go back inside.

CHAPTER SIX

MADELINE

Another week has passed and everything seems to be back to normal again. Well, almost normal. There is still an air of confusion running through town as to what caused the blackout. I've heard from a couple of library patrons that there are even some people who refuse to leave their houses out of fear that it might happen again. They've locked themselves in and won't answer the door or their phones. I can't imagine that it does any good to isolate yourself from people who are in the same boat as you.

I have a set work schedule once more, and today just happens to be my day off. Mrs. Donaldson needs me to mow her lawn, so I will have to do that later, but right now I'm relaxing in my recliner, with a cat on my lap and a book in my hand.

After reading for a while, I set my book down and grab the TV remote. I want to check again for a news station. There still haven't been any stations on the air, but I keep checking every now and then. I've tried to find the news websites that I would visit regularly, but they're still down, too. The cell towers have not been fixed, either. Even though things are back to normal here in the small town of Amherst, I'm not sure how things are going in the big cities.

Holy buckets, there's a news channel on!

"We are bringing you news live today from O'Hare airport in Chicago, Illinois. Mechanics have been working non-stop to get the remaining airplanes up and running. Tragically, the number of casualties appear to be astronomical! We are still uncertain just how many airplanes went down, but things are not looking good . . . "

I find myself sitting at the edge of my seat, chewing on my cuticles. Midnight is now sitting on the floor giving me a dirty look since she was so rudely kicked off my lap. I knew things were going to be bad. I just didn't know how bad!

They cut to a commercial. Really?! It feels like the world is ending, but they still have time for commercials? I stand up and start pacing around my living room waiting for them to be over.

The news show comes back on with a different news reporter.

"I am standing here on Interstate 41 outside of Milwaukee, Wisconsin. As you can see behind me, clean-up crews are still pulling cars out of ditches and cleaning up debris. They have enlisted the help of volunteers for the time being. There is a lot of work that still needs to be done before the main highways will be useable. If you are interested in volunteering . . . "

A blue car suddenly comes barreling out of nowhere right toward the news reporter. Just before it hits him, he looks over his shoulder and does a perfectly executed back flip right over the top of the car! The camera cuts out and the screen goes black.

They return to the stunned news anchors in the studio.

"Wow! That was amazing! We just got word that nobody was hurt."

I know I must look like a deer caught in someone's headlights. I shake my head and force myself to breathe again. That was one of the most amazing, yet frightening, things I've ever seen on live television. I'm shaken out of my stupor when my phone starts ringing.

"Hello?"

"Hey, Goose! Did you happen to be watching the news just now?"

"Yeah! That was amazing!"

"I have no idea how he did that! It was like watching a movie. Wow!" She pauses a moment. "Anyway, I was calling to see if you would like to come over for lunch on Saturday. Matthew said he would try to be here."

"Sure. What time?"

"Get here around eleven and you can help me prepare."

"What are you making for lunch?"

"A beef roast, mashed potatoes, green beans, and dinner rolls. I thought we could top it off with chocolate cake for dessert."

"Sounds great!" My mom is an amazing cook. Plus, it's a free meal, so win-win.

"How have you been feeling, Goose?"

"I've been just fine. Why?"

"Well, your father and I have been having days where we haven't been feeling too well."

"That stinks. Now that you mention it, I was talking to Elizabeth the other day and she told me that she has moments where she feels a bit off. Not like herself. Of course, I joked with her that she might be pregnant, but she says she doesn't think so. She has been having this feeling off and on since the blackout."

"Yes, that's how we've been feeling too. We've just been writing it off as old age," my mom says with a chuckle.

"Oh stop! You guys are not that old."

My parents are in their fifties. They are not that old, but I hate the thought of them getting older. They've always seemed so strong and bullet-proof that I just can't wrap my mind around that changing.

"Thanks, dear. So, you're sure you're feeling well?"

"Perfectly fine. I've even been riding my bike around town instead of driving and it feels great."

"That's wonderful! Maybe a cute guy will see you riding around town and ask you on a date."

I roll my eyes and sigh. "Maybe, Mom. I'm in no rush."

"I know. I'm just looking forward to being a grandma, is all."

Suddenly, I hear a hard bump against the wall I share with Mrs. Donaldson.

"What the . . . ? Mom, I need to get going. I'll see you on Saturday!"

"Love you, Goose. Bye."

I put my shoes on and go over to Mrs. Donaldson's place. I knock on the front door and hear her call out, "Just a second!"

Mrs. Donaldson answers the door. Her face is red and shiny with sweat.

"Are you all right?!"

She furrows her eyebrows at me and responds, "Of course, dear. Why?"

"I heard a loud thump on our connecting wall and I came to check on you. You look flushed. Is everything okay?"

"Absolutely! I had a burst of energy and decided to change my bedroom around. I didn't like where my furniture was, but it's better now," she says with a big smile.

As I look at her face, I suddenly notice something funny. She seems to have fewer wrinkles than I remember.

"You did what?! Mrs. Donaldson, you should have called me over here to do that for you! I would hate for you to hurt yourself!"

"It wasn't a problem at all. Most of my furniture has castors anyway, so they roll nice and easy. I've been having days where I don't feel right, but today I feel wonderful. I decided to do something with it."

"Well, that's good. But next time, maybe you should call me over to help you."

She gives me a pat on the cheek with one hand and grabs my hand with her other to give me a reassuring squeeze. She squeezes my hand pretty tightly for someone suffering from arthritis.

"Ow! You've got quite a grip there!"

"Oh! I'm sorry dear! That's the second time today I grabbed something harder than I thought I could. I almost broke a glass while washing dishes."

"Really? How's your arthritis been lately?"

"Funny thing is, I've been having more pain free days than ever before. I don't know what I've changed, but I'm really liking it," she says with a twinkle in her eye.

This is hard to process. How is it possible that her debilitating arthritis suddenly allows her to have enough strength to squeeze my hand so tightly and almost break a glass? And is that a few dark hairs I see mixed in with her full head of white hair?

"If you need anything, Mrs. Donaldson, don't hesitate to ask. I think I'm going to get started on your lawn since I'm here."

"Of course, dear. You are such a sweet girl. Thank you for helping this old lady out with so much. I don't know what I would do without you as my neighbor."

I smile and head out to start mowing.

As I walk out to the garage to get the lawn mower, I spot my neighbor, Ian, checking his mail. I'm glad to see he's doing okay.

"Hi, Ian! Beautiful day, isn't it?"

Man, I wish I had something more interesting to talk about than the weather.

He looks up at me and gives me one of those smiles that makes my heart skip a beat.

"Beautiful, indeed. Mowing the lawn for Mrs. Donaldson today? She mentioned that you would be doing it soon," He says, walking over to talk. He has a slight Scottish accent and I absolutely love it.

"Yes, but . . . " I step closer to him so Mrs. Donaldson can't hear me through her open windows. Our arms rub lightly against each other for a moment, causing instant goosebumps. I push the excitement down and clear my throat before talking "She is acting a bit strange. I hope she's going to be all right."

"Strange, how? Does she seem ill?" he asks, genuinely interested.

"No, actually, she seems the healthiest I have ever seen her. It's almost like she's getting younger. I must be crazy," I chuckle nervously, hoping he doesn't agree with me.

"I don't think you're crazy," he says, looking me straight in the eyes.

I smile and can feel my face blush. It doesn't take much to make me blush.

He looks down at his watch, "I should probably get back inside, though. I need to get ready for work. Hey, one of these days, when we're both free, we should go out for a coffee."

"Sure, that would be nice," I say, giving my best convincing smile. I hate coffee! But I would be willing to choke down a cup if it meant listening to him talk for a while.

I watch as he walks back inside, and then I head into Mrs. Donaldson's garage to get the old, push mower out. I'm pretty sure this thing is ancient, but it still works and Mrs. Donaldson doesn't want to part with it. She told me that she thinks about her husband every time she sees this little, red lawn mower. That, in and of itself, is a good enough reason to keep it around.

I push the mower out in the lawn to get it started.

One pull.

Two pulls.

Three pulls.

Come on, you darn lawn mower! Start!

Four.

Five.

I stop to catch my breath. I swear, trying to start this mower takes more energy than actually mowing the lawn.

Mrs. Donaldson peeks her head out of the door.

"Everything okay, Madeline dear?"

"Yeah. Just having a fight with the lawn mower again."

She steps out of her door and walks down the sidewalk to me.

"Here, let me try. I'm feeling lucky today."

Before I can protest, she scoots me out of the way, and with one quick, powerful tug, she gets it started!

I just stand there, staring at her. What in the world is happening?

"See! I just knew it would start for me." She gives me a pat on my shoulder and shuffles her way back in the house, humming to herself.

CHAPTER SEVEN

MADELINE

It's Saturday. I hop in my Jeep to head over to my parents' house for lunch. I'm glad to have my Wrangler in working order again. The bike rides were good for me, but my Jeep is so much more convenient.

There's Ian, working on his car. The hood is up and he's leaning over the engine. Just as I start to drive past, he stands up and looks my way. I give him a big smile and wave and get one in return. I sure hope he asks me out for that coffee soon.

I get to my parents' house a little early. Good. I like being early; so does Matthew. He's already here.

I let myself into their quaint, ranch-style home and head straight for the kitchen in back. It is slightly outdated, with wall paper and counter tops that look like they are from the 1970s but it is the house I grew up in, so I hardly even notice. It feels like home to me.

"Hi, Mom."

I give her a quick hug and sit on a stool at the counter.

"Where are Dad and Matthew?"

"In the living room, 'waxing philosophical' with one another. Their words, not mine. Your father loves it when Matthew visits. He can finally talk to someone who understands him," she says, looking slightly dispirited.

"Don't sell yourself short, Mom. You're smart, too. Where do you think I learned all my mad cooking skills from?" I ask with a smile. I know that it sometimes bothers her that my dad is a little sharper intellectually. She often has a hard time keeping up in conversations between Dad and Matthew, but I can never understand half of what they are saying, either.

"Not the same but thanks anyway."

"What would you like me to do to help get lunch ready?"

"You can peel the potatoes," she answers, pointing to the bag of potatoes by the sink.

I walk around the sickly, avocado-green counter to get the bag of potatoes and the paring knife.

"So, how has work been at the library?" my mom asks.

"Just fine. Mrs. Yates has needed me to fill in for her a little extra this week. She said she hasn't been feeling well. The extra money definitely helps, though."

"I'm sure it does. I heard that it might take a while for the economy to catch back up after what happened. The airlines alone are going to take a long time to recover."

"True. It's pretty scary, really. The news said that there have been tens of thousands of deaths reported from all over the world in the air plane crashes alone, and they're still counting," I say, shaking my head.

"Jeez! And that's not counting the deaths from the car accidents."

I decide to change the subject. Mom is starting to look a little worked up. "So, anyway, I was thinking about having you and Dad over on one of my days off. I thought it would be nice to make you supper for a change," I say, starting to peel a potato.

"Sounds like a good plan, as long as you are willing to make your chicken gnocchi soup for me."

"Deal! But you have to bring dessert. Make sure it's something chocolate."

Crap! I just cut myself with the knife. I grab a paper towel and hold it on my thumb without looking at how bad the cut is.

"You okay, Goose?"

"I think so. I'm afraid to check."

"Charles! Could you please come in here? Madeline just cut her thumb," my mom calls out.

My dad is a certified First Responder. He is good with this sort of stuff. He comes in the kitchen and gently grabs my hand.

"Let's see it."

I feel a funny tingling sensation in my injured hand as I am about to lift the paper towel off my thumb. Great. Did I hit a nerve or something? My dad leads me over to the sink and sticks my thumb under running water. The blood washes off, but there is nothing there. No cut anywhere to be seen.

"What . . . what just happened? I felt my hand get tingly when you grabbed me."

My dad seems spooked, and his face suddenly looks ashen.

"I assure you, Madeline, I don't know," he says and then pauses for a moment. "Funny thing is, I nicked myself shaving this morning, but when I washed the shaving cream off, I didn't see anything either."

My mom walks over to my dad and takes his face into her hands. She turns it from side to side, checking out his chin.

"Hmm. Nothing but handsomeness all over the place," she says with a wink, clearly trying to calm him down. It seems to work.

"Thanks, Marie. Well, did you need me for anything else, ladies? Matthew and I were just talking about what he has been doing in the lab."

"Nope. Thank you," I say.

I walk back to my seat, trying to wrap my mind around what just happened. I suddenly remember the guy jumping over the car and the little boy throwing the football farther than I thought he should. Not to mention the odd stuff with Mrs. Donaldson. There seems to be some strange things going on. I think I am going to have to start writing some of this stuff down.

"That was weird, Mom. I know this sounds crazy, but I think Dad healed me somehow."

"Don't be silly. Maybe you didn't really cut yourself that badly," she says, skeptically.

"But there is no cut on my hand at all! There was blood, so I should have some kind of wound."

"True . . . I'll keep an eye on your father and let you know if anything else bizarre happens," she says making light of it.

I take a deep breath, attempting to calm my thoughts. I'm having a hard time trying to make sense of it all. How is it even possible that I don't have a cut anywhere?

"So, I was just talking to Beatrice," my mother starts, using that tone of voice she always uses when she's about to tell me about some young man she thinks would be perfect for me. "You remember Beatrice, right? I think you met her once when we had a barbeque back in . . . oh, what year was that? Gosh, it's got to have been ten years ago now. Anyway, she's an old friend of mine from high school. She told me her son is in college to become a pharmacist. She says he's unattached. I told her that maybe we could set something up for you and him to meet."

And here we go again!

"Good grief, Mom. How many times do I have to tell you, I don't mind being single right now," I say, getting slightly annoyed.

She sighs, "I know, Goose. I just know how happy I am to be married to your father, and I want the same happiness for you. You and your brother mean so much to me. It would do my heart good to see you both fall in love with someone." She quickly turns to check on the roast in the oven.

I saw tears starting to form in her eyes. My mother is kind of a sap. I hate it when she cries. Sheesh! I hope she doesn't get tears on the roast.

"Fine. I didn't want to mention anything because I don't know if it's going to turn out to be anything," I huff.

"What?" she asks, her eyes lighting up.

"My neighbor Ian made mention that he would like to take me out for coffee sometime when we're both free."

My mother starts squealing and jumping up and down with delight. I look up from the potato I'm peeling and see that she is holding onto the pan of meat she was just checking on, without an oven mitt!

"Oh my God, Mom! Your hand!"

She stops jumping and looks at what she's doing. She quickly lets go of the roasting pan and looks at her palm. I rush over to her to look too, and there are no marks at all.

"That should have burned you, Mom! Are you okay?"

"It would seem so. Honest to goodness, I didn't feel anything!" she says, staring at her hand in disbelief.

"Dad! Matthew! Come in the kitchen!"

I need us all to sit down and talk.

"What's the matter, Mads?" Matthew asks.

"I know this sounds crazy, but first it seems that Dad healed my hand just by touching me, and now Mom was just holding onto the roasting pan without an oven mitt, and she didn't even get burned. There is some freaky stuff going on here that we need to figure out!"

"Really, Marie? Why were you holding onto the roasting pan without an oven mitt?" my father asks.

"I didn't do it on purpose. Madeline was just telling me that she has a potential date. I got overly excited, and I wasn't paying attention to what I was doing."

"You have a date?" my dad asks me with a big smile.

"Maybe, but we're getting off topic here. All of this is starting to freak me out. There have been other incidents that I've witnessed and can't come up with an explanation for either."

"Like what?" Matthew asks.

"Well, to start off, a little four-year-old throwing a ball a whole lot farther than he should have been able to."

"Maybe he has been practicing. Perhaps he's a prodigy," suggests Matthew.

"Fine, but what about the newscaster that did a perfect back flip as a car was speeding towards him?"

"Easy! He might have martial arts training and is capable of doing those things. Or he does free running in his spare time. He could be a ninja like me," Matthew jokes.

Mr. Know-it-all is starting to frustrate me. It doesn't seem like any of this is strange to him.

"Okay, well explain to me how Mrs. Donaldson seems to be getting younger and her arthritis is suddenly healing. She appears to have fewer wrinkles, and black hair is growing back in her snow-white hair. She was also able to start the push mower I was struggling with, in just one tug!"

"That could easily be achieved by a good vitamin regimen. Never underestimate the power of vitamins, Mads," Matthew says with a chuckle.

"Am I the only one who thinks all of this is messed up?"

Everyone just looks at me.

"I don't know what to say, Goose. Sure it's strange, but Matthew made some good points." Oh good. She's siding with Matthew once again. "I had just washed my hands before I checked on the roast. The water from my hands could have protected me," my mom suggests.

"Not for that long, Mom. And what about Dad?"

"Well, I . . . "

Just then the doorbell rings.

"UPS man is here. You got a package." Matthew says, as he takes a drink of his soda.

"How could you possibly know that?" I ask.

There are two walls separating us from the solid wood front door. Sure, Matthew is facing that direction, but there are no windows to look through.

Matthew looks kind of confused. He looks back and forth between all of us. "Well, Mads. You're not going to like this, but I saw him."

"What do you mean, 'you saw him'? That's impossible!"

This is insane. I feel like I've walked into the twilight zone!

"I can't really explain it. Somehow, I could see the UPS man put the package down and walk away. It was as though I was looking out a window at him."

"Come on, Matthew. You had reasons for all the other crazy things I listed. What's the logical explanation for you looking through the wall?" I ask, needling him a bit.

"I don't know." Matthew responds, shaking his head slowly.

Matthew looks freaked out now, too. Good. I'm not the only one. My mom pats his arm comfortingly.

My dad declares, "All right, maybe we need to do some tests to see if we can recreate these strange anomalies."

"What do you suggest, dear?" my mom asks.

"Well, why don't you see if you can touch something hot again without getting hurt and if you do, I can try to heal you?"

"You want me to go grab the hot roasting pan again?" my mom asks, kind of worried.

"No, I don't mean you should grab it with your whole hand. Maybe just touch it with a finger. That way, it won't cause serious damage," he suggests.

"All right."

She walks over to the oven. We all follow her. She opens the door, takes a deep breath, and gently taps the roasting pan with the tip of her finger.

"Nothing."

"Try again for a little longer this time," my dad insists.

I can't help but think this is all insanity. Interesting and a bit exciting, sure, but I am freaked out and beyond confused.

My mom puts her finger on the pan and holds it there. Nothing. She puts two fingers and soon she has her whole hand on the roasting pan.

58

"Nothing. I don't feel any of it!" She stares at her hand, and sees that it's perfectly fine.

Matthew looks like he is about to collapse.

"You okay, Matthew? What's wrong?" I ask.

"Umm, yeah. I think. I don't know. I'm pretty sure I just saw Mom's heart, and it was racing really fast!" he says, shaking his head.

"You saw mom's what!?"

"Her heart. I was watching her closely and suddenly, I was looking inside of her."

"Madeline, dear, why don't you have a seat at the counter next to Matthew?" my dad suggests. "You don't look so good."

He's right. I'm about to keel over right here.

"Okay. So, we have established that you can touch hot things without getting burned. I wonder if you have the healing . . . ability . . . or whatever is going on, like me. Matthew, we will address your . . . ability . . . in a moment," my dad says.

"I have an idea," my mom says as she walks over to the knives. "How about I make a small cut on my hand and we can see if I can heal it."

My dad hesitates and then says, "All right. I don't like it, but for the sake of the test."

My mom grabs a sharp knife, holds it to the palm of her left hand, and makes a quick slice across it.

"Ow! Good gravy that hurt!" she shouts.

Blood instantly starts running out of the wound. She walks to the sink to drop the knife in and run water across the cut.

"Let's see," my dad says, as he makes his way toward her.

She takes her hand out of the water and blood starts running out of the wound again.

"I don't think I can make it stop and it stings like a bugger!" she says.

My dad takes her hand between his and closes his eyes, like he is concentrating hard.

Suddenly, my mom says, "Oh! It's tingly and really itchy!"

My dad opens his eyes and let's go of Mom's hand. Her cut is gone.

My mom turns her hand this way and that, taking a good look at it. She gives my father a look of awe and then gives him a big kiss.

"This is amazing! How are you guys doing this?" I ask.

"I have no explanation for you. All I can say is that I have been feeling strange lately. Like a tingling sensation throughout my body, but I just ignored it," my dad says.

"I have felt the same thing," Matthew says "Like something is coursing throughout my body, but mainly by my eyes. I just wrote it off as the beginnings of a migraine. Have you been feeling anything like this, Mads? Maybe it runs in the family." Matthew smirks.

"No, I've felt just fine. Nothing weird at all."

"Why don't we go in the living room and check the news. Maybe there is something going on elsewhere. Perhaps we're not the only ones," my father suggests.

"I think I'm going to order some pizza. I don't feel like cooking right now and we can just use the roast during the week," my mom says.

I have a seat on the couch. My dad turns on the news and we watch it for a while. From what I can tell, life as we know it will never be the same.

The news report is a compilation of amateur videos people took of strange things going on across the country.

One video shows a teenage boy juggling what looks like ten balls, but he's not touching any of them. He's just holds his hands out in front of him and the balls fall toward his outstretched hand, then go shooting back up in the air, a lot like when the same polarity of magnets repels one another.

The next video is a little girl playing in a yard, and wherever she puts her hand, flowers and plants grow to her giggling delight.

There are videos of a person disappearing then reappearing twenty yards away, an elderly man dropping his cane and taking off running so fast that you can barely see him, and one of a toddler solving complex equations.

Finally, the pizza shows up. We turn off the TV, eat in stunned silence, and then I decide I want to just be home. This is all too much to take.

CHAPTER EIGHT

VINCENT

"I gotta take a leak," Pete says, getting up from the kitchen table that's covered with old newspapers and notes.

"What's wrong with you, man?" Frank asks.

"What?"

"This is like the fifth piss break you've taken in the last hour."

"It's none of your damn business," Pete says, hurrying off to the bathroom.

Frank shakes his head. "You okay there, Vinny?"

Vincent looks up from the spot on the table he has been staring at, and glares at Frank. He doesn't allow anyone to call him "Vinny" except for his ex-wife.

"I told you not to call me that," Vincent says.

"What . . . Vinny?" Frank says, pushing his luck, like he always does.

Vincent punches Frank's shoulder, directly on the bandage covering the still healing gunshot wound.

"Ow! You effin' jerk!" Frank says, grimacing in pain.

"Guys, knock it off! We've got business to deal with," Pete says, sitting back down at the table. "As I was saying, things are gettin' weird. Just yesterday I watched a little old lady pick up the front end of her car and drag it away from the curb so she could pull out. There's somethin' goin' on that smells a little fishy. The government's behind this, I know it."

"Is everything a conspiracy with you?" Vincent asks, moodily.

"Yeah? Hey, you're either one of us or your one of them. You know the government's run by power hungry idiots that go lookin' for fights. One of these days, somebody is gonna teach those pigs a lesson," Pete yells, slamming his fist on the table for emphasis.

"What other stuff you think you been seein' happening?" Vincent asks.

"Frankie here says that he's been havin' some sort of weird dreams. Like he can tell the future or somethin'," Pete adds.

"Yeah, man. This mornin', I knew that Pete was gonna offer me a beer before he even said anything."

"So you dream about gettin' offered a beer?" Vincent asks, skeptically.

"No. It's other stuff too. I saw this little kid outside, while I was lookin' out the window, and I had a strong case of déjà vu. I had a sudden urge to tell him to get outta the road. That nagging feeling wouldn't go away, so I opened the window and yelled at him to get outta there and sure enough, just as he runs up on the sidewalk, a bus comes barreling down the road, doin' about eighty. The kid woulda been roadkill if I hadn't warned him!" Frank says, face looking pale. Pete pats Frank on the shoulder.

"The other day, I got a call from my cousin in Nevada. He says he seen a whole lotta military vehicles drivin' out to the dessert," says Pete.

"Did he get a look at what they're doin' out there?" Frank asks, suddenly intrigued.

"No. He says a sandstorm kicked up outta nowhere and he had to leave. I bet they got security measures that could do that."

"They probably do. I'm thinkin' they did somethin' to us that made us all go to sleep so they could launch a probe or drones or somethin' to spy on everyone. They wanna know what we're all doin'. We ain't got no privacy. Sick . . . " Frank says.

"If we do find out the government's behind the event that caused everyone to fall asleep, I'm gonna kill every last rat bastard that had anything to do with it. Maggie was only four. I had to watch my little girl get lowered into the ground in a coffin. They're gonna pay for it!" Vincent yells, while scratching at his face.

"We'll help ya, buddy," Pete offers. "I know it's gotta be the government behind it. They want to control us. Like I've said before, all they gotta do is slip somethin' into our water or food supply and nobody would know till it's too late."

"Yeah. That could be it! Maybe they got a food supply out on a base in the desert that they're poisoning with a mind control drug. Then they're gonna spread it around and get us all to eat it and start makin' us do stuff we don't wanna do. Maybe we should start growin' our own food."

"You can't grow Twinkies and pork rinds, Frank," Pete teases, patting Frank's plump belly. Frank slaps Pete's hand away and gives him a not-so-nice hand gesture. For a moment, Vincent chuckles.

"Do you guys got any chap stick or lotion or somethin'? I can't stop itching!" Vincent asks, scratching at his scalp. His lips are cracked and bleeding.

"I'll check while I'm in the bathroom," Pete offers.

"Dude, is he taking another whiz?" Frank asks, scratching at the back of his hands.

Vincent looks at his arms and sees red patches of dry skin, which is odd. It's late summer. The weather outside is hot and humid, but the air in their apartment seems unreasonably dry. He puts his hand down on the Formica table to get up to open the window. A giant spark shoots from his fingertip.

"Damn it, it's dry in here," Vincent comments. He pushes the window up and props it open with a broken piece of broom handle.

"Here. I found this," Pete says, coming back into the kitchen. He hands a half empty bottle of lotion to Vincent.

Vincent starts lathering up his arms with the lotion. Frank grabs the bottle and does the same.

"Need some?" Frank offers to Pete.

"Nah. I'm good," Pete says.

Vincent looks at Pete's arms and face. He looks perfectly fine. As a matter of fact, his dark tanned skin seems to be glistening in the sunlight. Even his chocolate brown eyes seem to be more watery than normal. Pete's features have always reminded Vincent of a rat: watery eyes, pointy nose, and buck teeth. It sometimes disgusts him so much, he has to look away so he doesn't slap him.

"As I was sayin', we need to start making a plan. The government's plotting somethin'. They want to take over and we ain't gonna let 'em get us. I say we stock up on some more guns and lay low. We watch and wait for the right time to strike. They ain't controllin' me!" Pete says.

Vincent walks to the fridge to grab a beer in hopes of quenching his dry throat, but just as he's about to reach for the fridge handle, a large spark arcs from his pointer finger to the handle.

"Did you guys see that?" Vincent asks, bewildered. "That was the biggest static shock I ever saw in my life!"

"It's too damn dry in here," Frank complains, scratching at his face. "I feel like my skin's about to split open."

"I don't know what the hell you two girls keep goin' on about. It ain't dry. My shirt's soaked and here . . . look at this," Pete says, laying his hand palm down on top of a piece of newspaper. When he lifts it up, there is a perfect wet handprint left.

"What the hell?" Vincent utters, looking at the handprint.

"Guys, go turn on the news. There's a report on you need to see," Frank says, with his eyes closed. His eyeballs are moving rapidly under the lids as though he's watching something.

"This is a joke, right?" Vincent asks, freaked out.

"I told ya, this keeps happenin' to me. I don't know why. Just go check out the news," Frank says, spooked.

They all get up from the table and Pete takes yet another bathroom break. Frank and Vincent flop on the couch and turn on the news.

Pete joins them and they stare at the screen as they see video after video of people being able to do strange and amazing things.

"See! What'd I tell ya? Crazy stuff's happenin'," Frank says, shaking his head vigorously, causing his double chin to wag.

"Maybe you're right. I mean, we all woke up and didn't know how we got to where we were," Vincent says, shuddering as he remembered the dirty cell toilet. "Ya think we got the same thing as all those people?"

"You know, maybe the government didn't poison us with something for mind control, after all. I betcha they poisoned us with something to give us powers and then their gonna weed out certain abilities," Pete answers. "It looks like everyone's got their own special skills."

"Yeah! What if they want to find people who got weaponizable skills? Who can be made into super soldiers. They're probably lookin' for somethin' specific," Frank says.

"Well, Frankie here seems like he might be a good candidate, with his powers of dreamin' the future or whatever it is he can do. Why don't you go turn yourself in there, Frank? See what they do to you," Vincent taunts. He goes to slap Frank on the back and a spark shoots from his palm, burning a hole in Frank's shirt.

"Ow! Damn it, Vincent! Watch what you're doin'!" Frank yells.

"I don't like this. I don't like this one bit. Frankie's tellin' the future, and now Vincent's shooting lightning from his hands. . . " Pete says, shaken.

"Pete's pissin' like a race horse," Vincent smirks.

"Shut up, you prick! I'm serious!" Pete says.

"Hey, maybe he's got that thing . . . ya know. Something you learn in science class as a kid. Water suckin' into something else . . . I think it starts with an 'o' . . . " Frank says, his scruffy face scrunched in thought.

"Oasis . . . no, no . . . Osmosis." Vincent offers.

"Yeah! Yeah, that's it. Maybe Pete's got osmosis goin' on. You're wet and everything, including us, is so dry. Dude, you're suckin' the moisture right outta the air."

"I guess that explains the constant need to pee . . . What the hell? You guys get cool powers and I just suck the water outta the air?" Pete says, looking genuinely jealous.

"Look, I think you're on to something, Pete, 'bout the government behind this. We better keep our powers a secret. 'Specially you, Frank. Don't go tryin' to pick up chicks with your cool mind games. The government could be listenin' in on us right now," Vincent says looking around the apartment suspiciously.

"We should get word out. We should warn people to not let the government use 'em as super soldiers," Frank says. "I'll put somethin' out on our webpage."

Pete nods his head and gets up to join Frank at the computer. Vincent lays his head back on the couch and closes his eyes, his mind immediately starts picturing his little girl; her long, curly raven hair, the dainty freckles that run along the bridge of her nose, her startling baby blue eyes. He lets tears run down his face as a fresh wave of grief washes over him. *I'm going to make them pay, even if it kills me.* He takes a deep breath and tries to relax. As he does, he feels a tingling course through his entire body.

CHAPTER NINE

MADELINE

On my way home, I stop to pick up a journal so that I can start writing things down. I need to make a list of everything going on to keep my mind clear. I walk in the duplex, put my purse away, and grab a bottle of water. I go to my bedroom, where my computer is, and see my cats lazing around on my bed. Oh, if only life were that simple. I give them both a scratch behind the ears and sit down at my computer desk.

First things first. I need to know if this is a world-wide thing. I type in "superpowers" in the search engine. Silly me. Of course, all the super-hero movies and comics are going to pop up first. I should have known. Okay, how about "superpowers in the news." The first thing that comes up is the news channel report that I just watched. I don't need to see that again.

Scroll.

Scroll.

Aha! Here's an article from China.

A man with the ability to walk through walls, started holding hostages in the vault at the Industrial & Commercial Bank of China. One of the hostages, who claims to have the ability to speak telepathically, alerted a police officer outside. A SWAT team showed up moments later and was able to get inside the bank by using a member of the SWAT team who could make portals through solid walls. Just as the SWAT team member was making a portal into the vault, the captor snuck his way behind the SWAT team and started shooting them. After killing two members, he shot at a third, but didn't realize that this member was bullet proof. He was apprehended, but who knows how they are going to be able to keep him in jail.

I write down "telepathy, ability to walk through walls, portal maker, and bullet proof" in my journal. And that is just the beginning.

An hour later I have four solid pages of superpowers from all over the world written down. Age doesn't seem to matter, either. There are reports all the way from small babies to the elderly. The level of superpowers differs, too. There are a lot that seem to be pretty simple or not entirely useful. The ability to drink as much alcohol as you can possibly consume and never get drunk seems like a fun party trick, but otherwise useless. Then there is a guy who is able to make his nose hair grow insanely long on command. Gross!

I decide to check out some videos on YouTube, and I am not disappointed. I'm sure some of these could be faked, but at this point I'm not willing to rule anything out.

I watch a video someone took of their little boy by an ocean. He is running across the sandy beach toward the sparkling water, and as soon as he reaches the water, he just keeps going, right on top without sinking! The mom drops the camera in the sand and we see a sideways glimpse of her feet running toward her son to catch him. We can't see what is going on, but you can hear the mom screaming the little boys' name, and then all-of-a-sudden, there is a shrill shriek that cracks the camera lens and the video cuts out.

I scroll down to the comments under the video and the consensus seems to be that the mom was the one who shrieked so loud she broke the lens.

There is a video from New Zealand of a man hiking up a mountain on a beautiful, sunshiny day with a camera attached to his head. We can see from his point of view that it's treacherous terrain. He takes a path that is winding its way around a steep cliff, but then a rock lets loose and his foot slips, causing him to fall over the edge. I gasp and hold my breath, thinking I'm about to witness this man's demise, as the ground is getting closer at a sickening rate. But then he abruptly stops. I think that maybe he got snagged on a tree branch or something, but from what I can tell, the ground starts shrinking away. The man appears to be flying! After only a few short seconds, the view of the ground is blocked by clouds.

The next video I watch is of an attractive young lady who apparently has the ability to persuade people into giving her whatever she wants. All she has to do is touch their arm and tell them to do something and they do it. That could turn out to be quite dangerous.

I watch videos until I finally have to stop because my eyes hurt. I look at the clock. I have been at it for five hours already!

I do a quick search to find out if there is anyone out there that does not have any new superpowers. Nothing so far. Not even a group on Facebook. I decide to make one. I name it "Powerless."

Finally, I check out how people are explaining where these powers came from.

The first article I find is some conspiracy theorist's take:

. . . the government has poisoned us all to find the people who would best make super soldiers. They plan on gathering up the people with powers that will benefit their agenda and control them to do their bidding.

I laugh. Even with everyone suddenly getting new abilities, it seems a little far-fetched.

Another article states:

The world of X-Men has become reality. All of humanity has mutated at the same time.

Nope. I don't believe that one either.

Hmm. Here is one written by an astronomer. He has been watching the stars closely over the last few years and now one of the stars seems to have disappeared out of the sky. There is no solid answer for the disappearance, but the word *supernova* is mentioned. That word seems to stand out in my mind, so I write it down in my journal, deciding that I will look it up later. I need to get to bed now. I can barely keep my eyes open. This was a highly successful evening, and I look forward to digging deeper. But what I really want to know is if I have any special abilities. Maybe tomorrow I should do some tests to find out.

CHAPTER TEN

MADELINE

My alarm startles me awake. I was having that dream again where I'm standing in my yard, everything flashes blue, and then I blackout. I rub my eyes and then stand up to stretch. I need to get ready for work.

I grab a quick breakfast, take care of my cats, throw on some jeans and a nice blouse, and head for work.

I walk into the library and Mrs. Yates is there.

"Good morning, Mrs. Yates. Please don't tell me I got the day mixed up and it isn't my day to work."

"Oh no, Madeline. It's your day to work. I just needed to do some research. I'm not really sure what's going on with me."

"What do you mean?"

"Well, the other day, I was shopping at the mall and a group of Asian women walked past me talking to each other in Chinese. Another customer leans over and says 'Don't you wish you could understand what they were saying? I sometimes wonder if they are making fun of us.' But the funny thing is, I could understand what they were saying. They were just talking about what other stores they wanted to shop at."

"You understood them, but you don't know how to speak Chinese?" I ask, trying to understand.

"Exactly! I have never mastered any language other than English. Plus, last night my husband was watching Star Trek, and when the Klingons were talking, I understood them too. And that's a made-up language! I feel like I'm losing my mind!"

I decided to tell her all about my research and the abilities my family just discovered they had.

"Really? Now that you mention it, I do recall some odd behavior. I drove past the high school yesterday and saw a girl climbing up the side of the building with nothing but her bare hands. I just brushed it off thinking I must have been seeing it wrong. And have you driven past King Cone recently? I can't drive past the place anymore! Every time I go near it, I get this sudden urgency to eat ice cream and can't shake it until I have a scoop. It must be the same for everyone else, because there is always a huge line. The ice cream has always been good, but there is something weird going on there." Mrs. Yates pauses for a second. "You know what? Maybe my ability is omni-linguism!"

"I'm sorry. Omni-what?"

"Omni-linguism. It is the ability to speak and understand all languages."

She slips into the foreign language section and opens a Korean language book. "Madeline! I can understand all of this!" she yells out. "Oh, this is so exciting!"

She comes to the checkout desk with a stack of books. I can't help but smile with her. She seems so thrilled with her newfound ability.

The library closes at two o'clock today. I have decided that I'm going to go to the park and try to figure out what my ability is. It seems like everyone in the world has new powers except me so far. I don't want to be the only one without a special power. After living my whole life in the shadow of my genius brother, always being compared to him and always coming up short, I don't want to be overshadowed once again. This would be on a much grander scale.

Before I leave the library, I head over to the foreign language section and grab a book. Nope. I don't understand any of it. Oh well.

As I am driving to the park, I have a sudden urge to get a cone of my favorite ice cream. I look to my left and realize I'm approaching King Cone. Mrs. Yates was right. The desire is so strong, I feel something bad is going to happen if I don't have any. I stop and wait in the long line for half an hour to get some salted caramel ice cream. I hop back in my Jeep to continue with my plan. My goodness, this ice cream is good! I need to add King Cone to my list of superpowers.

I get to the park and walk until I have found what feels like a secluded area. I really don't want anyone to watch me. I sit down with the notebook and make a list of some things I could try:

Possible Abilities

1. Speak to/hear animals
2. Grow plants by touching ground
3. Run super fast
4. Climbing
5. Teleportation
6. Voice control (sing well, high scream, or booming voice)
7. Walk on water
8. Turn into something

9. Control the elements
10. Fly

I think this is enough things to try for now. I have a seat under a tree. I look to see if there is anyone around. Nope. I put my hands, palm down on the ground, close my eyes, and concentrate on making a violet pop out of the grass.

Grow. Grow violet. Come on. Grow!

I open my eyes to see if it worked. It did not. Well, I can cross that one off my list. Oh! There's a squirrel over there. Let's see if I can talk to it. Wait . . . what do I say to a squirrel?

I start off quiet. "Hello. My name is Madeline."

The squirrel just keeps rummaging through the leaves on the ground looking for acorns.

I say a little louder, "What are you doing there, Mr. Squirrel?"

Man, I feel like an idiot. The squirrel just keeps on ignoring me. I stand up and decide to walk closer to it.

"I won't hurt you. Come here, little squirrel."

The squirrel stops what it's doing and runs up the nearest tree. I can hear him start chittering at me. Well, I definitely don't speak squirrel. There's a robin in the next tree. I'll try talking to it.

"Hello, pretty bird. You have a nice song."

The robin flies away. I guess I can cross that one off my list, too.

The next item on my list is "run super fast". I set my notebook at the base of a tree. Again, I look around to make sure nobody is watching. All clear. I stretch my legs a bit and take off running. Okay, anytime now super speed. Nope. Just my normal speed of averageness. I stop to catch my breath. Next up:

Possible Abilities

1. ~~Speak to/hear animals~~
2. ~~Grow plants by touching ground~~
3. ~~Run super fast~~
4. Climbing
5. Teleportation
6. Voice control (sing well, high scream, booming voice???)
7. Walk on water
8. Turn into something
9. Control the elements
10. Fly

Climbing. I wrote this one down because I have never been good at climbing trees. Even as a kid, Matthew would always be able to climb higher and faster than me. It might have to do with my uneasy feelings of heights.

I look around until I find a good climbing tree. There's one about twenty yards away with lots of branches closely spaced. I walk over and set down my notebook. I grab onto the lowest branch, take a deep breath, and hoist myself up.

I make it about six branches up, when I realize that this is not my forte. Not only am I moving at the pace of a sloth, but I am also starting to shake and becoming dizzy. I climb back down, praying I don't fall on my butt. Up next: teleportation.

I'm not sure how I'm going to attempt this one. I remember reading a book about a school of magic where the kids were trying to get from one point to the other just by imagining themselves doing it. So I pick a spot between two trees to focus on.

Okay, Madeline. You can do this. You are here and you want yourself to be right there. Just focus. Focus!

Fifteen seconds later, I'm still standing in the same spot. Darn!

Oops! While I was focusing so hard on trying to be in that other spot, someone walked by and saw me. Now they are staring at me.

I wave. "Sorry! I was just . . . daydreaming." I feel my face blush, and I hurry back to my notebook. I glance up to see if they left. They're gone.

I would have thought it would be easier to figure out what I can do. It seems like it came so easy to everyone else.

I sit down with my notebook. I'm getting a bit discouraged and start considering giving it up for the day, but this next one should be simple enough to test, so I give it a go. I'm an okay singer but not great. I tend to sing a lot, so I'm familiar with how I sound. I decide to try singing "Amazing Grace," one of the prettiest songs I know.

It sounds about the same as usual. I try booming my voice instead. I fill my lungs with air and start talking real low. I increase my volume. Nope. That's not it either.

I remember the video of the mom cracking the camera lens with her shriek, so I go into the bathroom in the park to see if there's a mirror. There just happens to be one. I know I should probably do this at my house, but I'm curious. I'll pay them back if it works. I check under the door of the stalls to see if there are any ladies in here.

I'm alone.

I yell at the top of my lungs.

Ow! I successfully hurt my ears, but the mirror is still intact.

Well, my throat is raw now. Frustration is starting to set in. I have tried and failed half of my list already and it's getting old.

I head down to the lake to sit and think about it all. I start to relax while I watch the setting sun reflect its orange light on the smooth water. After I sit and watch it for a while, I find that I can't help myself, and decide to try one more thing on my list. I walk up to the water's edge and attempt to step on the surface, but my foot plunges straight down and now my sock and shoe are soaking wet. It's time to go home.

At bedtime, I find that I can't go to sleep. My failed attempts at discovering my ability keeps running through my mind. I still have some things I could try. I don't know if I should, though. I lie in bed for another half an hour, waiting for sleep to come, but it won't. Maybe I need to slake my curiosity.

I slide out of bed and grab the notebook to see what's next on the list.

Possible Abilities

1. Speak to/hear animals
2. Grow plants by touching ground
3. Run super fast
4. Climbing
5. Teleportation
6. Voice control (sing well, high scream, booming voice???)
7. Walk on water
8. Turn into something

9. Control the elements
10. Fly

I'm not sure what I should try to turn myself into. Maybe I will be like Mystique from X-men and will be able change myself into someone else. The first person I think of is Elizabeth, so I try to change myself into her. I close my eyes and think hard about her dark, long hair, her shorter stature, her skinny frame.

After a while, I realize that I feel exactly the same. I look at my hands. Yup! Same freckly hands I always have. Okay, how about an animal?

My favorite animal is the tiger. I picture a tiger in my head. The beauty, the grace, the ferociousness. I open my eyes. Still a human.

I'm starting to get mad again.

I look back at my list. There are only two more things on it: control the elements and fly. I go to the kitchen sink, plug the drain, and start filling it up with water. Once it's full, I put my hand right above the water to see if I can make it do anything.

 Of course not.

I hold both of my hands out in front of me like Storm does in the X-Men movies. Once again, nothing!

I grab a box of matches out of my junk drawer. I strike one, and hold my hand by it, willing it to do something! Fine! Maybe I need to touch the fire to be able to control it. I strike another match and hold my palm over the flame.

Ouch! I just burned myself! Now there is a red welt on my hand. I am so angry right now, I can feel heat radiating off my face. I can't remember the last time I was this mad. I throw all caution to the wind. I am going to fly! This has to be my power.

I go outside to my backyard and find a good climbing tree. Maybe I just have to want something bad enough.

Once I'm at the top, I will myself to open my eyes and look around. I can't be scared of heights if my power is flying.

Okay, Madeline! Fly! Just imagine yourself being weightless and gliding over the tops of the trees. You can do this! This has to be it! Focus and...Fly!!!!

I let go of the tree, but fear takes over. I think better of what I am about to do.

Wait! Maybe I shouldn't do this! I scramble to grab onto the branch but it slips out of my hand.

I feel the sensation of falling, then land with a crunch that causes a bright flash of light, and I wake up, lying in a hospital bed.

CHAPTER ELEVEN

MADELINE

Pain.

Excruciating pain.

I hurt everywhere. I open my eyes and my mom's face is the first thing I see.

"She's waking up!" she cries out. I see my dad and Matthew walk over to my bed.

My mom is sitting next to me, holding my hand and stroking my hair.

"Where am I?" I croak. I wince at the pain. It hurts to breathe, let alone talk.

"You're at Saint Michael's Hospital, Goose. Mrs. Donaldson found you laying in a heap at the bottom of a tree outside your duplex and called an ambulance. You've been unconscious for a whole day. Do you remember what happened?" my mom asks.

I close my eyes, trying hard to control the pain. I do remember what happened. They are not going to like it. I decide to tell them what I did anyway. This is going to take a while, since I can barely even breathe.

"I decided . . . to try to find my special power. I made a list . . . and by the time I got to the end of my list, I was enraged . . . and I wasn't thinking clearly. I was going to try to fly . . .

but obviously, it didn't work . . . I fell from the top of a tree. I feel like I was hit by a truck. So, tell me . . . How bad is it?"

Just then the doctor walks into the room. He's tall and lanky with salt and pepper hair. Attractive but aged.

"There she is. Well, young lady, you took quite a beating. You have three fractured ribs, a fractured tibia, and a whole lot of cuts and bruises. You're going to need to wear a cast for a while, I'm afraid," he says, looking over my chart.

Great. Just what I needed. Not only am I ordinary, with no special powers like everyone else in the world, but now I'm temporarily disabled.

Weak.

Useless.

I start crying.

"It's going to be all right, Mads," Matthew says.

"Oh . . . what would you know! Your whole life . . . you've been perfect! I have never been able to measure up to . . . your accomplishments! This is just one more thing . . . to add to my list of . . . failures!" I finish, panting shallow and fast.

Matthew looks completely dejected and leaves the hospital room.

Everyone is quiet for a moment, clearly stunned. I start to feel guilty for telling Matthew off, but he deserves it. I have spent my whole life trying to be as good as him, and now he has a superpower to top it off.

I can see that my mom has something to say, but is waiting for the doctor to leave. Every time I make eye contact, she starts shooting daggers at me. I'm not sure which is worse, the pain from my broken bones or the fear of my mother's wrath.

The doctor is the first to break the awkward silence.

"It's a bit dark in here. Let me turn on a light for you," he offers, which he proceeds to do without touching any switches.

One more superpower to add to my list. Not sure the list even matters anymore at this point.

The doctor finishes checking my bandages, gives me another dose of medication for the pain, and promises that he will be back to check on me.

As soon as the doctor leaves, my mom lets me know what she thinks.

"Madeline! How dare you treat your brother like that? Why do you keep trying to compare yourself to Matthew? You're acting childish! It's not his fault he was born with a higher intellect —"

"Great, so now you're calling me stupid? Thanks, Mom . . . I don't already feel bad enough as it is," I snap.

"That's not what I meant, and you know it. . ."

"Enough of this," my dad says, scooting my mom out of the way. "Madeline, what were you thinking!?" my dad asks, gesturing to my broken leg. Clearly, he's not impressed with my desire to test my limits and discover what I'm capable of.

I cast my eyes down in shame.

"I'm sorry, Dad . . . I was just caught up trying to figure out my super ability. Speaking of abilities . . . do you think you could heal my broken bones?" I choke out.

"I'll see if I can heal your fractured ribs, so you can breathe easier, but I'm leaving your leg the way it is. Consider it a reminder not to do something so foolish again."

He places his hand on my side, which hurts me so bad, I cry out in pain. Then he closes his eyes and focuses. My side starts to tingle, it gets annoyingly itchy, and then I don't feel anything. I must have bumped my head pretty hard when I fell out of the tree, though. I thought for a second there that I saw the veins in his arm glowing blue, but now they are back to normal.

I take a pain-free deep breath.

"Thank you, Dad. I am so sorry for risking my life like that. I'm just trying to understand why I don't have abilities like everyone else."

My dad leans over and kisses me on the forehead. Then he walks back to the other side of the room and sits down. He still looks upset. I wanted to plead for him to fix my broken leg too, but I'm not going to push it right now. Just then Matthew walks back into the room. He heads straight over by my dad and has a seat. He still looks hurt. My mom gives me a meaningful look, trying to get me to apologize to him.

"Hey, Matthew." I don't feel like apologizing right now, but maybe if I ask him for his expertise on something, it will take his mind off my outburst. "I was looking up theories about how everyone acquired these unnatural abilities and one of the articles used the word supernova. I vaguely remember learning about them, but I was wondering if you know more about it."

"Well, I saw on the news that a group of astronomers are meeting this week to discuss some of their findings and calculations. There is talk that one of the stars closest to Earth seems to be missing. If a supernova happened at that distance from the Earth, who knows what kind of repercussions that would have," Matthew responds, his sadness being replaced with a bit of excitement.

"Interesting. But what is a supernova, Matthew?" my mom interjects.

"A supernova is the explosive death of a star. I don't know a whole lot about it, since I am a biology major, but I am looking forward to what the reports say."

"Let me know what you find out," I say. "I would be interested learning anything about these new-found superpowers. And maybe we can hunt down an answer as to why I don't have any."

I can feel disappointment and anger seeping in again. And perhaps a bit of jealousy.

"No problem, Mads." Then Matthew turns to the closed door and says, "Come on in, Elizabeth," two seconds before we hear her knock.

I subtly roll my eyes at my brother's x-ray vision. I know my mom is right. I'm being childish. I guess I just feel like an outcast now.

Elizabeth comes in the room, holding a bouquet of flowers.

"Hi, Madeline. Hello, everyone. Is this an okay time to visit?" she asks, looking around at our solemn faces.

"Absolutely, dear. We were just going to go down to the cafeteria and have a bite to eat," my mom says. "We'll be back in a little while, Goose." She gives me a quick kiss on the top of my head, and they leave so I can catch up with Elizabeth.

"I'm so sorry you're hurt, Madeline. What happened?" she asks, as she places the flowers on the table by the window and has a seat by my bed.

Elizabeth patiently listens to me tell the whole story. It takes quite a while to tell. I feel a little foolish recounting all the silly things I did. When I'm finally done, I let out a deep sigh.

"I guess I don't blame you. I think I probably would have done the same thing, but who knows? You might not be the only one in the world without powers. Maybe there are other people out there who don't have them, either."

"Maybe," I say, skeptically. "Have you discovered what you can do yet?" I ask, although I'm not sure I really want to hear her answer.

"I have. I try not to do it too often, though, because it feels rather odd that we wake up and suddenly everyone has supernatural powers. I discovered that I can make force fields. I can put up a field that blocks out sound from coming in or going out. I'm pretty sure it can protect me from objects, too."

"That's pretty cool," I admit.

Suddenly, Elizabeth looks sad.

"Yeah, but like I said, I don't really use it that often. I had to use it last night, though. Philip was upsetting me, and I needed to block him out. Things are not great, Madeline." Elizabeth starts to cry.

"What's the matter? Did he hurt you?"

I don't trust Philip. I know he loves Elizabeth, but the way he treats me makes me wonder what he is like when he gets angry at her. I once picked Elizabeth up and we went out hiking for the day without telling him where we were going. We grabbed some supper after we were done, and we lost track of time. I ended up dropping her off at her house pretty late. Philip called me the next day when Elizabeth had gone out shopping and completely reamed me out, like some sort of over protective parent, telling me it was irresponsible and that in the future I'm to okay any outings with him first. I really wanted to punch him in the face after that. I chose to not tell Elizabeth about it. If he treats her well, who am I to be a thorn in their marriage?

"No, no, he didn't hurt me. I know he would never hurt me. He has become an adrenaline junkie, though. His power is that he gets incredibly strong whenever he has an adrenaline rush. He loves the feeling of the strength, so he has been seeking out dangerous activities. But it comes with a side effect. He gets angry. The more intense the adrenaline and strength are, the angrier he becomes."

"Are you saying he becomes the Hulk?"

We both laugh and Elizabeth wipes a tear off her cheek.

"Not quite. He doesn't turn into a big, green giant. But he just keeps searching out activities that will give him a rush without thinking twice about how I feel about it or about how angry he gets afterward. Last night he got home from cliff diving with some friends and he started screaming at me for leaving dishes in the sink. I got a little freaked out, so I put up a field so that I couldn't hear him yelling. He finally snapped out of it and apologized for scaring me."

"Wow, Elizabeth. I'm so sorry. Maybe you should consider taking a break from him. At least until he can control this?"

"That's the thing, Madeline," she looks at the floor, hesitating. "I just found out yesterday morning that . . . I'm pregnant."

"Oh my goodness, Elizabeth! I'm so happy for you!" I say, jumping up in my bed. Big mistake! I wince from the pain that shoots through my leg.

I have mixed feelings about her news. I truly am happy that she is pregnant, but then again, I'm not so sure after hearing about Philip's new powers.

She smiles. "Thanks, Madeline."

I hear the door handle turn. My family must be back from lunch.

I look towards the door and suddenly everything looks shimmery. I look back at Elizabeth. We are encased in the shimmery substance. You can see through it but everything looks distorted, like when you see heat waves rising off a hot road. She must be using a force field.

"Don't tell anyone about my news yet! I haven't told anyone but you."

I nod. I feel so special to be the first to know. It's going to be hard not to tell my mom, but I'll try. She releases the field.

"Hey, Goose. We brought you back some fries and a shake. We didn't like the looks of the hospital food, so we went out to eat. Sorry we didn't grab anything for you, Elizabeth dear. We didn't know if you would still be here or not."

"No problem. I actually have to head out, anyway. Take care, Madeline. I'll call you soon."

She gives me a gentle hug and leaves.

I eat my food with my family in silence, but then I feel wiped out.

"I don't mean to be rude to you guys, but I'm feeling exhausted right now. I think I need to get some sleep."

"You're not being rude, Madeline. You just went through a traumatic experience. Get all the sleep you need," my dad reassures me.

I fall asleep almost instantly. I have that dream again. The one where I'm in my front yard, there is a deep rumbling sound and then everything flashes blue. Only this time, other people are outside with me. When the blue flash hits, the people tense up like they're in pain, all the veins in their bodies glow blue and they crumple to the ground, unconscious.

CHAPTER TWELVE

VINCENT

"**I** need to run home and grab some stuff," Vincent says.

"Dude, you just broke outta jail. You can't go wanderin' around. You'll get caught," Pete warns.

"I know what I'm doin'."

"Fine. Go. But when your sorry ass is thrown back in jail, don't come cryin' to me," Pete says, rolling his eye.

Vincent slams the door behind him and makes his way out to the old brown beater car he shares with his friends. It's a rundown Cadillac he picked up for cheap years ago, though the gas to run it isn't so cheap.

I need my pictures of Maggie.

He drives across town to his house. His parents' left it to him when they died. It used to be a beautiful three-bedroom house, with a manicured lawn, and a picket fence, but it's not much to look at anymore. Vincent hasn't spent much time and effort to keep it up. It has chipping paint, broken shutters, and a rusty metal roof, but it's home and Vincent is glad to have it. It's nice to have a place to be on his own for a while. He likes the work that he does with Pete and Frank, but they certainly know how to get on his nerves and sometimes he just needs to be alone.

He parks the car in the driveway and heads to the front door.

Somethin's wrong.

The front door is not only unlocked, but it's open just a crack. He pushes the door wide open, standing off to the side, out of sight.

I wish I brought a gun.

He takes a chance and peeks his head around the corner. He doesn't see anyone. He steps into the house and finds his floors littered with his belongings: books scattered, cushions strewn all over, broken picture frames . . .

He rushes to check on his favorite picture. It's a picture of him holding Maggie, right after she was born. He likes the way he looks in it because the happiness of holding his new baby girl shines brightly in his eyes. There is nothing in life that has brought him more happiness, than being a dad. He finds the picture still in the broken frame, unscathed.

He continues rummaging through his things, carefully removing the pictures he came here for. Suddenly, he hears a loud bang in the back yard. He stands up and makes his way to the back of the house, carefully stepping over the broken glass. He looks out the window of his back door and sees a man wearing a ski mask carrying a large sack over his shoulder, trying to climb over his fence.

He's stealing my stuff!

Vincent whips open the door.

"Drop it!" Vincent yells.

The thief turns and looks at Vincent. He puts the bag down slowly and raises his hands as though he's under arrest. Without warning, he claps his hands together in front of him, sending a shock wave that knocks Vincent off his feet.

Vincent hits the ground with a crunch, as the windows shatter behind him.

What the hell!?

The thief picks up the bag and continues his attempt to climb over the fence.

Two can play at this game.

Vincent gets his bearings back and stands up. He lifts his hands out in front of him, pointing his palms towards the perpetrator. He's not sure what he's going to do, he can feel the electricity flowing through his arms. Large lightning bolts shoot out of his hands, hitting the thief in the back. The thief falls to the ground with a moan. The back of his shirt is burned away and smoking, leaving his charred skin exposed

Vincent looks at his palms incredulously.

Did I just do that?

He tries it again, pointing his palms towards the ground. A lightning bolt streaks out of his hand and leaves a smoldering hole in the yard.

He runs over to the thief and picks up the bag of his stuff. He gives the thief a good kick to the head, rendering him unconscious.

He goes back into the house and quickly collects the rest of the pictures he came here for.

I'll clean this place up some other time.

He goes to the car to head back to the apartment.

I can't wait to show Frank and Pete what I can do!

CHAPTER THIRTEEN

MADELINE

"In you go, Madeline," my dad says, helping me through my front door. I got released from the hospital today. Looks like I'll have to wear a cast for the next eight weeks. Life is going to be difficult maneuvering around with these blasted crutches. Why did I do something so foolish? It's all I can do to keep myself from crying. I'm not usually this big of a sissy, but lately I can't decide if I want to cry or be angry at the world.

"Where would you like to be, your recliner or bed?"

"I'll sit in my recliner. You know, you could just fix my leg and then you wouldn't have to help me anymore."

"Sorry, Madeline. My mind is made up. I love you, but I feel like your actions need consequences. I wouldn't want you trying something even more foolish, thinking I'm just going to swoop in and save the day."

"Fine," I huff, rolling my eyes.

I get myself settled in. My mom brings me a glass of water and my bottle of pain killers.

"Would you like me to fix you something to eat, Goose?" my mom asks, stroking my hair.

"No, thanks. I think I'll just sit here and take a nap," I say, as I lean my head back and close my eyes, holding back the tears. I don't want my parents to think there is something wrong. They have lives to get back to. They have done so much for me already.

"Knock, knock!" someone calls out in a sing-songy voice. Mrs. Donaldson walks around the corner into the living room. At least, I think it is Mrs. Donaldson. Half of her hair is jet black and she looks about twenty years younger.

"Mrs. Donaldson? Is that really you? What are you doing here?"

"I talked to your parents, and I offered to help take care of you. You have been so selfless in helping me over the last couple of years. I thought I should repay the favor," she says with a twinkle in her eye.

This is so messed up. The dear old lady, riddled with arthritis, hardly able to walk or hold a pencil, is now going to take care of me? I feel a sense of humiliation and shame. I got myself in this situation, and I feel like I'm being a burden to everyone I care about.

"You don't have to do that, Mrs. Donaldson. Really. I can take care of myself."

"Nonsense, dear! You rest up and before you know it, you'll be as right as rain."

I nod my head. Looks like there's no talking her out of it. My parents say goodbye and reassure me that they will stop by in a couple of days. After they leave, I call Mrs. Yates at the library to ask when she needs me to return to work. She tells me that I should take a week or two to rest up, even though I practically plead with her to come back to work. Anything is better than just sitting here feeling miserable.

For the next hour, I hear Mrs. Donaldson bustling around my place, cleaning and humming to herself. She offers to get me something to eat, but I have no appetite. She gets me a ham sandwich, anyway, telling me that I should really eat something. I say thank you but leave it untouched on the end table.

"Well, Madeline dear. I got your place all tidied up. If you need anything, anything at all, do not hesitate to call me, and that's an order!" she says with a smile.

I don't plan on doing that. I don't plan on asking anyone for help. Everyone can just stay away from me with their perfect little superpowers and unbroken legs. I sigh.

"Thank you, Mrs. Donaldson. I appreciate your help," I manage to choke out with what I hope is a smile.

As soon as Mrs. Donaldson leaves, I let the tears flow. I feel silly for feeling like this. I'm just so angry that I'm the only one in the whole world that doesn't have some kind of power. I have lived with feelings of inadequacy my whole life, because of Matthew, and now I am being bested by a little old lady.

I feel singled out.

Lonely.

And now my leg is broken, and I'm in pain most of the time. This is the first time I've been alone since it happened, and now I feel nature calling. I have to learn how to take care of myself sometime. I put down the footrest, grab my crutches, and manage to stand myself up with a grunt. I take it slow, going sideways through doorways, and finally make it to the bathroom. The whole process takes a whole lot longer than it used to, but I feel better that I can at least maneuver around my place by myself.

And so it goes for the next few days. Mrs. Donaldson comes over to check on me and does some light cleaning. I worry that my cats are going to start loving her more, now that she is cleaning their cat box and feeding them every day. I still feel a lot of pain, but I make myself get up and move around. I am bored out of my mind! I think I'll call Mrs. Yates and ask her to bring over some fresh library books to keep me occupied.

The next morning, I manage to get myself dressed and out to the living room before I hear the knock on the door. I'm sure my hair probably looks messy, even though I ran a brush through it. I wouldn't know. I don't look in the mirror much anymore. It is easier to not see myself in this pitiful state. It kept making me so angry that I had to stop before I broke the mirror out of disgust.

"Hi, Mrs. Donaldson. You don't have to come over this morning, there's not much for you to . . . " and I stop midsentence because it's not Mrs. Donaldson. It's Ian walking around the corner into my living room.

"Hi, Madeline. Is this a bad time? Sorry I didn't call first," he says with a smile.

I blink a few times to make sure my eyes are working properly. Am I really seeing this gorgeous man standing in my duplex? His light brown hair is disheveled in just the perfect way. He's wearing a black fitted t-shirt with a Metallica ninja star on the front, jeans ripped at the knees, and sandals. Yes. It has to be real. There is no way my mind would give me such a wonderful vision in the dark state it has been in lately. As soon as I deem this reality, I start running my fingers through my hair, hoping it looks okay.

"Ian? Why are you here? I mean, what brings you to my home?" Oh goodness. I'm so nervous I might throw up.

"Mrs. Donaldson caught me outside and told me that you could use a different visitor. I've been meaning to come over, anyway, just to see how you're doing. May I sit down?"

"Oh, yes! Please, have a seat. I would offer to get you something, but it might be quicker if you got it for yourself," I chuckle.

I try to shift myself to sit up straighter, but it causes a sharp pain to shoot through my broken leg. I cringe.

"Oh, are you okay? Do you need me to get you anything?"

"I'm fine, thanks. So, how have you been, Ian?"

"I've been doing pretty good. My stomach hurts a little right now," Ian chuckles a bit, rubbing his hand over his stomach. "I had to run some errands this morning and every time I drove past King Cone, I had an uncontrollable urge to get some ice cream. After the third time, my stomach started to hurt, but I just couldn't resist it."

"I know what you mean. That place has some crazy vibes going on there."

Ian smiles and changes the subject, "You know . . . you didn't have to break your leg just to get out of going out for a coffee with me," he says with a smile.

I blush. "That's not it at all! I was actually looking forward to it."

"Great! How about dinner Friday night instead?"

"Sounds wonderful," I say.

We are both quiet for a moment. I keep glancing at him, wondering how he doesn't already have a girlfriend, and why he would be interested in me. Especially now. Now that I have a broken leg and I'm not endowed with any super-ability. But, of course, he doesn't know that. I wonder what his ability is.

"What's wrong, Madeline? I mean other than your leg, obviously. You seem a little down."

He is either highly perceptive or I look as miserable as I feel, even though I'm trying my hardest to put on a good face.

"I was just curious. Have you noticed the new abilities everyone in the world suddenly has?"

"Yeah, I noticed. It's hard not to."

"Well, that's how I hurt my leg," I start to say, but stop. I stare at the floor trying to make up my mind whether I want to reveal the story of my idiocy to him.

"How? Were you fighting crime or something and broke your leg?" he asks.

I look up at him and see him smiling at me.

"No. Nothing nearly as heroic or brave as that," I reply. I take a deep breath in and let it out slowly. "I was so desperate to find my ability, I climbed a tree and was going to jump to see if I could fly. I thought better of it too late and I fell. Not having a superpower was bringing back bad memories from my childhood. My brother, Matthew, has always been the best at everything. He is a genius. I was never able to keep up with his perfect behavior, his perfect grades, or his brilliance. And now he has a superpower and I don't. I just feel so alone." A sense of shame washes over me again as I say it. I feel embarrassed at having shared so much.

And I start to cry. Darn it, Madeline! Showing weakness in front of Ian. Stupid.

He walks over to my chair, lifts my chin, and wipes away a tear with his thumb.

"You're not alone, Madeline. I don't have any superpowers either," he says, looking sad.

I stop crying immediately. "What? Are you serious? I thought I was the only one!"

He shakes his head no and gives me a sweet smile. I can't help suddenly feeling elated. I am not alone! It is even more awesome that it's Ian who doesn't have the special powers. Oh, this is so great!

"How have you been handling it? I mean, seeing everyone else have superpowers, knowing you don't? As you can see, I'm not handling it too well," I say, motioning to my leg. "In fact, lately, I have been dealing with a dark cloud over my head, so to speak." I give him a sheepish smile.

"Well, I just stopped watching the news, and I keep to myself mostly. It's hard feeling alone in the world, but now we have each other," he says, giving me a gentle touch on my shoulder, causing instant goose bumps. He walks back to the couch to sit.

"So, where do you want to go to eat on Friday? What kinds of food do you like, Madeline?"

"You should ask what kinds of food I do not like. It would be a much shorter list." I laugh. "Let's see . . . I like pizza, burgers, steak, chicken, pretty much anything. I'm not picky."

"How about sushi?"

"Now, that, I don't like."

"Good! I don't either." We both laugh.

We spend the next few hours having a wonderful time talking and joking around. We take turns asking questions to learn more about each other's likes and dislikes. We like the same kind of music: rock. He also likes cats, but he likes dogs more. Only not little dogs. Apparently, when he was a child, they owned a little dog that would constantly yip and bite at his ankles.

This was exactly what I needed to lift my spirits.

"Wow, it's getting late. I have to get to work soon," Ian says, checking his cell phone.

"I feel bad. I've never asked you where you work."

"That's okay. It's nothing special really. I'm a second shift maintenance worker for the foundry. It's dirty and loud there, but I like working on the machines. The pay and benefits are worth it, too."

"Well, it's good that you like what you do," I smile, and he nods his head.

"Is there anything I can get you before I go?"

"Not that I can think of. Oh wait! Maybe we should exchange phone numbers," I say, a little worried that I am being too forward.

"Of course. If you start feeling that 'black cloud' returning, just give me a call," he says as we program each other's numbers into our cell phones. "I'm looking forward to our date on Friday. How about I pick you up at six?"

"Sounds great!" I say, trying to stand up to see him out.

"You don't need to get uncomfortable for me. I can let myself out." He walks over to my chair, takes my hand in his, and gives it a quick kiss.

"See you soon, Madeline. Take care of yourself."

I feel like my heart is about to explode out of my chest. This guy is amazing!

CHAPTER FOURTEEN

MADELINE

I t felt like this week dragged by exceptionally slow, but Friday is finally here. I have been looking forward to this day so much that every time the depression tried to creep its way back in, I would just think about my conversation with Ian and our upcoming date. My mom called me yesterday, but I chose to keep my date with Ian secret for now. I am so nervous about tonight, I don't need her making things worse, trying to micromanage how I behave and what I should and shouldn't talk about. I'll let her know how things went afterwards.

I check the time eagerly. It's four o'clock. I decide to start getting myself ready. I'm not high maintenance and I never take two hours to get ready for anything, but I do have a broken leg, so I give myself this extra time cushion. Taking a bath is a lot of work, nowadays. Just trying to get myself in and out of the tub without causing too much damage can be quite the undertaking.

I finish getting ready and stand in front of my full-length mirror. Since Ian told me that he doesn't have any powers either, I am able to look at myself again. I know it's silly to base my self-worth on other people and their circumstances, but I just felt so alone.

Hmm. Other than my ghastly leg cast, I don't think I look too bad: Sleeveless black dress that hangs below the knee, a comfortable black dress shoe, hair pinned up, and just a little eye liner to make my green eyes stand out.

I finished getting ready with fifteen minutes to spare. I sit and wait nervously, watching the clock and picking at my cuticles. I consciously force myself to stop. The last thing I need is a bloody finger to deal with on my date.

About five minutes to six, I notice my leg is starting to ache badly. I grab my crutches and make it to the bathroom to take some pain killers, and before I know it, I hear a knock on my door.

I swallow the medicine and hurry as fast as I can, almost tripping myself when my crutch catches on the doorway. I answer the door and there's Ian, looking remarkable! He's wearing a navy-blue dress shirt tucked into khaki pants that look as though they were just ironed, and casual black dress shoes. He gelled his hair to look a little messy and the result is amazing.

"Wow, Madeline! You look beautiful."

I blush and return a compliment. He helps me out to his black sedan. Right away, I can tell that he takes good care of it. It's spotless and smells nice. I wonder if he keeps his place this clean. Maybe I'll find out someday.

"Nice car!"

"Thanks. It's getting up there in mileage. I was thinking about getting one of those new Dodge Challengers, but I'm not sure I want to commit to buying such an expensive car."

"If you do, you'll have to give me a ride sometime. Those cars look awesome."

"Sure thing! I didn't know you were into cars."

"Sort of. I appreciate how they look, but I am definitely not a mechanic. I usually take my Jeep in to a shop, even for an oil change."

"You don't have to do that. I can help you. I'm sort of a grease monkey. I enjoy working on machines. It is my job, after all."

"That would be wonderful. I'm always afraid that I'm getting ripped off whenever I take it in. I have no idea what parts are broken, so I feel like I can't question them when I get the bill. I will gladly ask for your help."

We arrive at the restaurant and Ian tells me to stay in the car. He walks around to open the door for me and helps me up. He gets my crutches out of the back, and we head toward the restaurant. I'm so glad that stores and restaurants are opening up again. So many were shut down for weeks after the event.

The restaurant has been beautifully decorated. There is a white lattice gazebo outside that has been adorned with sparkling clear lights and creeping vines. Blue and white flowers seem to be growing just about everywhere. A fountain stands next to the gazebo, adding a relaxing touch to the ambiance outside.

Once inside the dimly lit restaurant, I feel the same sense of relaxation. Candles flicker in the center of white clothed tables. The same blue and white flowers that are outside, have been planted in flower boxes at the top of each booth seat. We sit down and see that there are even blue cloth napkins, shaped like fans with brass holders in the middle. I'm so nervous. I'm not used to eating at such a fancy restaurant.

We get our menus and start searching for what we want to eat. I hate to admit it; I'm the kind of girl who likes deep fried food, so the appetizers are looking good to me. But I decide that I should eat something a little healthier, especially since I'm on a date.

"Do you know what you want to order?" Ian asks.

"Not yet. How about you?"

"I think I'm going to get the sirloin steak dinner."

That was what I was looking at, too, but I decide to order grilled chicken instead. I wonder if he is the kind of guy who wouldn't mind sharing a bite with me.

We set down our menus and Ian starts up the conversation. With all the superpowers being discovered all over the world, we get into a lively discussion about which comics are better: DC or Marvel. I am more of a Marvel girl, myself, but Ian is making a case for DC. I glance over to the middle of the room and stop midsentence. Ian sees what I'm looking at and watches too.

A balding, greasy looking man is sitting alone at a table. I can't believe I didn't notice him before because he certainly doesn't fit in here. He's wearing a stained, white t-shirt and ratty, camo shorts, reclining in his chair like he doesn't have a care in the world. We see food flying off other peoples' plates toward him. Then he grabs it in midair and eats it. When a couple get up to leave the restaurant, the tip they left on the table suddenly floats toward the man and he pockets it.

"I can't believe that guy!" I say.

"I wonder if the people working here are seeing this," says Ian.

The waiter comes back to our table to take our order. We tell the waiter what the man is doing, and he assures us that it will be taken care of.

We return to our discussion. "I think that guy must have telekinetic powers. That's a cool power, but obviously, he's choosing to use it for evil instead of good," I say.

"I hope it's okay to ask, but if you could have a superpower, what would you want it to be?" Ian asks me.

"I have thought about it a lot, actually, and I remember seeing a video of this little girl that made plants grow wherever she put her hand. I want a power where I can grow food plants. I mean, think of all the hungry people you could feed!"

"Wow," Ian says, looking down at the candle on the table. There is a moment of silence.

"Why? What would you want to be able to do?" I ask.

"No. It's stupid," he continues to avert his eyes.

"Oh, come on. Please?" I give him the most winning smile I can muster. He glances up at me. The red in his cheeks looks so adorable.

"Fine, but don't laugh. When I was little, I almost drowned. Ever since, I get kind of nervous around lakes and stuff. I would always fantasize about being able to breathe under water. So, I guess that's the super power I would want."

"Ah! Now I understand your love for Aquaman."

"Yeah. It's nothing as profound as feeding the hungry, but it has been my dream since I was a little boy."

"No, I get it," I say. I decide to change the subject. "I feel like I know so little about you, Ian. Do you have any siblings?"

"Nope, it's just me. My parents moved to the United States just before I was born. They didn't have a whole lot of money, and my dad worked hard to provide for our little family, but I had a happy childhood."

"That's good. I know this is a silly question, but do your parents happen to be from Scotland?"

"Yes, they are. I'm saving up to take a trip there someday. I want to learn more about my heritage."

"Awesome! That has always been one of my dream destinations. It looks so beautiful there, and I love the accent. Especially yours," I say, with a smile.

"Good. Maybe you could come with me," Ian says, giving me a sincere look.

Whoa! Did he really just ask me to go on a trip to Scotland with him? I wonder if he's serious. Seems a little fast. I'm not sure how to respond, so I just smile.

"Oh gosh, Madeline! I hope I wasn't being too forward!" Ian says, looking embarrassed.

"No worries. Maybe we should go on a second date first, though," I say with a wink.

Suddenly, we hear raised voices. We look over to the guy who was stealing things and there's a man dressed in a suit, asking him to leave. I think he must be the manager of the restaurant.

"Sir, we saw you stealing things. We cannot allow that kind of conduct in our facility. We are asking you kindly. Please, leave."

"No, thanks. I think I'll stay right here."

"Sir, you need to leave. Now."

"I said no."

The manager looks furious and starts to step toward the man but suddenly, the man holds his hand out in front of him and the manager's arm is twisted behind his back in an arm lock by some invisible force. By the look on the manager's face, it must be quite painful.

"I'm staying right here, and there is nothing you can do about it," the man says with a sneer.

He thrusts his hand forward, causing the manager to trip without even touching him. He puts his hands back down to his side and the manager's arm is released from the arm lock. The manager walks briskly away, rubbing his arm. The man leans back in his chair with a satisfied look on his face. The guy really creeps me out! As far as I can tell, he hasn't even looked in our direction. I hope it stays that way.

Shortly later, our food is brought out to us. It looks delicious. Ian even offers me a bite of his steak. This guy's a keeper. We are enjoying our food when a police officer walks into the restaurant. He steps up to the telekinetic man.

"Sir, you are going to have to come with me down to the station."

The man stands up, but suddenly the police officer's gun is out of his holster and pointed directly at the officer's head. The gun cocks in midair. The police officer looks completely shocked.

"No, officer. I believe it's you who needs to leave, and I will not be going with you."

The policeman puts his hands up in the air and starts backing up

"Sir, I don't want any trouble. Please, just put the gun down and I'll leave you alone."

The man takes a few steps to mirror the police officer's. The policeman turns around and runs out the door.

"I think it's time to go," Ian says.

Our waiter is walking close to our table, so Ian gets his attention and tells him that he wants to pay our bill. Ian hands the cash directly to the waiter, so that the telekinetic man doesn't have the chance to steal it. I grab my crutches and we make our way out of the restaurant as fast as we can.

I feel much safer once we pull up to my duplex.

"That was intense! What is the world coming to, that we can't even rely on the police for protection from guys like that?" I ask.

"I have no idea. Hey, are you going to be all right? You seem a little spooked," Ian asks.

I am a bit spooked. It suddenly seems like maybe it isn't such a great thing that people have these superpowers.

"I'll be fine. I just can't believe that happened."

Ian helps me out of the car and up to my front door.

"Thank you for the wonderful supper, even though the theatrics were a bit unnerving," I say with a smirk.

"I promise that next time I'll try to find a better place to take you."

"I'd like that."

He brushes a few stray hairs off my forehead and leans in for a kiss. I meet him halfway. I have never truly kissed anyone like this before. I kissed a boy in the seventh grade, but it was just a quick peck and I don't really count it, anyway. I didn't bother myself with boys in high school. Nobody seemed to want to date a girl who has a genius brother. They probably assumed I was a genius as well and that was too intimidating. He pulls away and I can still feel the warmth of his soft lips.

"I'll talk to you soon, Madeline."

He walks back to his car, and I can see that he is still smiling. I can't wait for our next date.

CHAPTER FIFTEEN

MADELINE

I wake up feeling the happiest I have felt in quite a while. It was the first night I didn't have my recurring dream about glowing blue explosions, and last night was one of the best nights I've had in a while, or maybe ever. Sure, there was a telekinetic klepto at the restaurant, my leg is still broken, and I don't have any superpowers, but neither does Ian, which makes him even more intriguing and desirable.

Maybe my mom is right. Maybe falling in love can bring insurmountable happiness. I've watched my parents over the years. Yes, they have disagreements. Yes, there are bad moments, and they've seen each other at their worst. Yet they still love each other. They still find happiness with each other. They've told me over the years that a key ingredient to a happy marriage is communication.

"Talk to each other about everything. Be honest and truthful."

"Let each other know how you feel about things, so that there won't be miscommunications that could easily have been avoided if you had just talked."

I'm so lost in thought and I almost miss the doorbell. Shoot! I'm not dressed yet. I throw on a bathrobe and hobble my way to the front door. I really hope it isn't Ian. . .

It's not.

"Good morning, Mrs. Donaldson! Sorry I'm not dressed yet, but you are welcome to come in if you want," I say with a big smile.

"My, my, Madeline, dear. You seem to be in a pleasant mood," Mrs. Donaldson says, returning a smile on her almost wrinkle-free face.

"Oh! Is it that noticeable?" I ask, with a sly grin.

"Well, not to sound harsh, dear, but you have been rather bitchy lately," she responds, turning to head towards the kitchen.

Whoa! I'm stunned for a moment. I don't believe I have ever heard her say anything worse than "crap" the one time she burned her cookies. I follow her into the kitchen where she's humming to herself and unloading my dishwasher.

"Did you just . . . ?"

"I take it your date went well with Ian?" she interrupts, as though she didn't just let slip a rather rude remark. I just shake my head a bit. Maybe I just imagined it.

"Oh, it was wonderful. I really like Ian. He even made it sound like he might ask me out on another date," I say, the smile creeping back on my face.

"Well, that's wonderful, dear. And who knows, maybe you'll finally get laid," she says, as she puts a plate away in the cupboard.

What is going on? I never would have guessed that my sweet, elderly neighbor would speak like this, especially to me.

"Mrs. Donaldson! Are you feeling all right?" I ask, a little flabbergasted.

"I'm feeling fine, dear. Why do you ask?"

"Well, you just said a couple of rather rude things to me."

"I did? I'm not sure what you are talking about," she said, looking slightly confused.

Just then, she reaches to put a plate away in the cupboard and her sleeve pulls up, revealing her arm. I see that her veins are bright blue, almost shining, under her pale skin.

"Your veins! Mrs. Donaldson, it looks like you're glowing!" I say as I hobble towards her.

"Oh, yes. I did notice that this morning. Seems rather odd, wouldn't you say?"

"Yes. Yes it does. Do you need to go see a doctor?"

"Whatever for? I've never felt better. My arthritis is pretty much gone, and I'm finally able to do things for myself again, without you always barging in," she says. She starts humming again and steps around me to take care of the cats. Just then the phone rings. I go to the other room to answer it. I'm just about in tears at how Mrs. Donaldson is treating me. And the funny thing is, she seems to not even know she's doing it.

"Hello?"

"Hey, Goose. I'm just calling to see how you are."

"I'm fine, I think."

"You think?"

"Yeah, Mrs. Donaldson is acting strange today. She has said a few rude things to me."

"That doesn't seem right. Are you sure you're hearing her correctly?"

"Yeah, but she doesn't even seem to realize she's doing it. She acted confused when I confronted her about it. Oh, and her veins are glowing blue."

"Glowing? Are you sure you haven't taken too many pain meds, Goose?"

"No, Mom. I was having an absolutely wonderful morning before she showed up and started acting weird. But I'm glad you called because I have something to tell you."

"What?"

"I went out on a date with my neighbor Ian last night. He's amazing. I really like him, Mom."

"That's wonderful! I'm so happy for you! Are you going to go out again?"

"He made mention of a second date, but nothing is figured out yet. Hopefully our next date will be less eventful."

"Less eventful? What do you mean?"

"There was a guy there at the restaurant that was stealing things with his telekinetic powers, and then pulled a gun on a police officer when he was asked to leave."

"What?! That's crazy! I'm glad you're okay!"

"Thanks, Mom. You know, suddenly superpowers don't seem to be all that great. If the police can't protect us from the bad guys, who will?"

"Maybe enough good people will stand up and fight for what's right. We could have some real live superheroes on our hands," she says, jokingly. "I take it you're feeling a little better about not having these powers?"

"Yeah, I guess so. It doesn't hurt that I'm not the only one."

"Really? What do you mean?"

"Ian told me that he doesn't have any superpowers either. I can't tell you how freeing it is to know that I'm not the only one."

"That's great, Goose! I would love for you to introduce us to this Ian next time we visit."

"Maybe. I don't want to push it. Perhaps I should go out on more dates with him before I introduce him to my parents," I laugh. "Oh! I gotta go. I'm getting another call. I'll talk to you later. Love you. Bye!"

I answer my call waiting. It's Matthew.

"Hey, Mads." he says. The tone in his voice indicates that he hasn't completely gotten over my outburst at the hospital.

"Hi, Matthew. Look, I'm sorry about yelling at you in the hospital. It wasn't right for me to lay into you like that. It's not your fault that you got a superpower and I didn't."

"It's okay. We'll just blame your crankiness on your broken leg," Matthew offers.

"Deal."

"I have some news for you."

"You got a girlfriend?" I say jokingly.

"You know, if I wanted to get hassled about a girlfriend, I would have called Mom."

"Sorry. Go on. You were saying?"

"There has been a breakthrough. The government has brought together a team of astronomers and scientists for a meeting about the current situation. Professor McGreggor was invited, and he told me what they discovered. The star that seemed to have gone missing did, in fact, go supernova. The radiation at that close of range wreaked havoc on anything and everything electrical. That's why everything shorted out."

Suddenly, I remember the dreams I've been having.

"Matthew, I think I've been having dreams about the supernova. In my dream I'm outside, there is a deep rumbling sound, it flashes blue, and then I blackout. Do you think it might be memories of what happened? Not just dreams?"

"It could be, Mads."

"Crazy."

"It gets even better. After some testing, they theorized that the radiation released from the supernova damaged everyone's plasma cells. This caused the plasma cells to produce an over-abundance of a special kind of paraprotein."

"Wait, what is a paraprotein?" I interrupt, confused. He tends to forget that I'm not majoring in biology, like he is.

"Paraproteins are a kind of protein that are found in the blood as a result of cancer or other diseases. In this case, they were formed because of the radiation. Do you know what plasma cells do?"

"No."

Matthew sighs, "Plasma cells create antibodies. Paraproteins are like antibodies, only they don't fight infection."

"So, what do they do?"

"Well, the condition that closely relates to what is happening to everyone is called monoclonal gammopathy of undetermined significance, or MGUS for short. Only, this new paraprotein that is being mass produced in our bodies is unlike anything we've seen before. We think that it might have something to do with the supernova radiation. We have more research to do to find out what exactly this new form of paraprotein does. I'll let you know as soon as we find out more."

"Thanks for keeping me in the loop, even though I might not understand all of it."

"You're welcome." He pauses a moment. "I should also add, Professor McGreggor told me that, so far, they have not documented a single person that doesn't have MGUS or a superpower. I'm sure more may turn up, eventually, but right now you are the only one without a power. If you don't mind,

I would like you to come down to the lab sometime so that we can walk over to the hospital and get a sample of your blood. The professor believes that having a sample from someone not affected could be helpful to understanding more about what has happened."

"I'm not the only one."

"What?"

"My neighbor, Ian, told me that he doesn't have any powers either."

Just then Mrs. Donaldson walks by and interrupts me.

"Well, I'll be going, dear."

"Thanks for all of your help!"

"Slave work is more like it," she mumbles, as she walks out my door.

What has gotten into her?

"Sorry about that, Matthew. Something strange is going on with Mrs. Donaldson. She has been quite blunt today. . ."

"That doesn't sound like her. She has always been so sweet," Matthew interrupts.

"And I noticed her veins glowing blue."

"Really? You know something? I noticed my veins glow blue the other day, too. I just chalked it up as something to do with my new 'eye sight.' But I feel perfectly fine."

"Well, Mrs. Donaldson says she feels fine, too. She doesn't even seem to notice when she is being snide. Be careful, Matthew. I would hate for you to become more of a jerk-face than you already are."

"Ha. . . ha. . ."

Just then I hear a knock.

"Someone's at the door. I should go. Thanks for calling and keeping me informed!"

"No problem. Talk to you later."

I put the phone back in my pocket and slowly make my way to the front door. This morning has been crazy, with so many calls and visits. Who could it be now?

I open the door. It's Elizabeth, sobbing so hard she can barely stand.

CHAPTER SIXTEEN

VINCENT

"I don't give a crap!" Vincent yells, sparks shooting out of his fingers.

"Well, ya should, Vince. I don't like the way your and Frank's veins are glowin'," Pete frets.

"Jeez. Are you sure your power ain't the ability to whine like a little wussy?" Vincent asks.

"Take a look at Frank over there," Pete says, pointing at Frank sleeping on the couch. "He's been usin' drugs to put himself to sleep so he can keep havin' them dreams. Look at his arms, Vince. He's practically glowin'! There have been more and more messed up crap goin' on from people with glowin' veins. I think it's makin' people crazy!"

"Eh. Frank's fine. I'm fine. Stop worryin'," Vincent says, staring down at his arms. "What about you? We can't even see your skin. You're always wear that stupid rain gear."

"I have to. I got sick of havin' to pee constantly and being damp all the time. The rain gear keeps the moisture away from my skin. It's hot though . . . " Pete says, flapping the green rain jacket to let some air under.

"I will give it to ya. There is some people acting crazy out there. I went to the liquor store to buy some brandy the other night, and some glowin' freak thought he could steal my wallet from across the store. I felt something move by my back pocket, and when I turned around, my wallet was flying through the air towards the guy. He didn't handle the lightning bolt to the forehead too well," Vincent says with a smirk. "While I was payin' for the booze, he got up off the floor and started muttering somethin' about me being Thor. He asked me to take him to Asgard. Frickin' nut!"

"Why'd you pay for the booze if you can shoot lightning? You could've just taken it. If the clerk said somethin', you could have shot him too," Pete says.

"We're supposed to be keepin' a low profile, remember? If I stole the booze, they coulda called the cops on me. We don't want our powers to be in the system. The less they know about us, the better."

Without warning, Frank starts yelling for them to come. They rush into the living room and see Frank sitting up, sweating, and breathing heavy.

"What'd you see?" Pete asks.

"It's hard to understand sometimes. I saw a building with a long line of people standing outside. They all had blue glowin' veins and some of them weren't right in the head. Mutterin' to themselves, smilin' like loons. But people who were coming out of the building looked normal. Their skin wasn't glowin' no more and they looked healthy."

"You sayin' their powers were gone?" Vincent asks.

Frank shrugs his meaty shoulders, "I don't know." He lays his head back down on the pillow and starts to doze off again.

"Well, if the powers were gone, why would people be so willin' to go give them up?" Pete asks.

"Don't you see? It's all a trick. The government poisoned us to give us these powers, not thinkin' it through on how they're gonna keep everyone under their control. Now they wanna take them away from us. To hell with them! They ain't takin' my powers away!" Vincent says, shooting a lightning bolt at the floor for effect.

"You don't know that their powers were gone. Maybe some scientists just found a way to make their veins stop glowin'. Maybe the government just brainwashed people into thinkin' they were getting' rid of the powers for some reason or nother and instead they're just loggin' people and their powers in a database and implanting trackers in them or somethin'," Pete says getting worked up. "Vince, why do you want to keep somethin' the government gave you, anyway?"

"Because they screwed up, that's why. I don't think they understood the depths of what they were getting themselves into. I can shoot lightning bolts! They gave me a weapon that I can use against them!" Vincent says, watching sparks shoot off his fingertips with satisfaction.

"I want to take down the government just as much as you do. . . " Pete stops when Vincent gives him a death glare. "Sorry, almost as much as you do, but we gotta be smart about it. We can't take them all out by shootin' lightning bolts at them. We're gonna wait for the right time to present itself."

"To hell with waiting! If Frank is right, and they try to take our powers away, I say we find a way to get our message across that they can't control us no more. We stop whatever it is they made from gettin' distributed. Let everyone keep their powers."

"And what if Frank is wrong? What if they didn't make somethin' to take our powers away?" Pete asks.

Frank's eyes pop back open to the sound of his name. "I ain't wrong, man. My dreams never are. There was a name in my dream, though. Some chick's name. Mary . . . Megan . . . Marcy . . . Gah! What was it? Mad . . . Madeline. Yeah, that sounds right."

"Who is she?" Pete asks.

"I don't know. A scientist maybe . . ." Frank says.

"Great. Some chick named Madeline. What good does that do us? Do you know what she looks like? Where she lives? A last name?" Vincent asks.

"No. Sorry. Just her first name. I'll see what I can find out as soon as I fall asleep again."

"Dude, this ain't healthy. I think you should take a break. Help us come up with a plan of attack while awake. Your veins are lookin' pretty bright, man," Pete says fearfully.

"I'm fine, mommy. There ain't nothin' wrong with me. Just let me do my thing," Frank says, picking up his bottle of sleeping pills. He pops three tablets in his mouth and swallows them down with a glass of water, then makes his way to the bedroom. Pete just watches shaking his head, worry etched across his face.

"He'll be fine," Vincent says, reassuringly. "Let him do it. He's more helpful with these visions than he was while awake. We gotta get more information, before we can really come up with a plan. And the only way we are going to get it is if Frank sees it happen."

"Fine. I hope he gets more information on this Madeline chick. What if she's the scientist behind what happened that gave us all powers?"

"Then we're gonna find her and take her out!" Vincent says.

"You sayin' you wanna kill her?" Pete asks, surprised.

"Hell, yes! If she's workin' for the government and she was part of this superpowers thing, she's gonna pay for what she did to my Maggie!"

"That's if Frank has more dreams about her," Pete says, glancing at the bedroom door. "I don't know. Maybe we should let them take our powers away."

"What? You're the one that's always yappin' about takin' down the government and now you're on their side?" Vincent asks in disbelief.

"I'm freaked out, man!"

"You're just bein' a jealous baby because you didn't get a cool power like Frank's or mine," Vincent says, holding his index fingers six inches apart and watching a lightning bolt jump between them.

"Whatever. You wanna keep your powers from the oh-so-trustworthy government? You go right ahead. But don't say I didn't warn you when things start goin' to hell. Everything goes wrong when the government's involved."

CHAPTER SEVENTEEN

MADELINE

"Elizabeth! What's wrong?"

I grab her elbow and try to help her stand up straight, which isn't easy with my dependence on my crutches. Her face is red and splotchy from crying. Tears are streaming down her cheeks. We make our way into the living room to sit on the couch.

"Oh, Madeline! It's so horrible," Elizabeth chokes out between sobs.

I hand her a box of tissues. She takes a moment to blow her nose and tries to settle down.

"What happened? Are you all right?"

"I'm fine. I am just so scared," she says, as fresh tears start pooling in her eyes again.

I put my arm around her shoulder and feel her shaking. She lays her head on my shoulder and cries until I don't think it is humanly possible to shed anymore tears. She finally takes a deep breath and starts talking.

"Philip is losing it! He's angry all the time now, not just after his adrenaline rushes. I can't have a conversation with him that doesn't end up in a shouting match."

"Oh, Elizabeth. I'm so sorry."

"That's why I'm here. We got into a fight about money. I bought myself a new pair of shoes that I didn't really need,

I just thought they were cute. He found them and started screaming at me about wasting his money." She stops to try to gather herself after the tears start flowing again.

"He said that if I wanted this junk, then maybe I should stop being worthless and get a job," she manages to say between sobs.

"Then he threw the shoes at me. I put up a force field and he started pounding on it, screaming while he did. I came over here once he stormed out of the house."

"Oh, dear. You are more than welcome to stay here as long as you like."

"Thanks, Madeline. I know I sound crazy, but his veins have been glowing blue. I noticed it a little when this all first began, but they're so bright now, they practically glow in the dark. I think my veins have glowed a little from time to time, but nothing like his. I'm so worried about him!"

"Do you think you should take him to the doctor or something?" I suggest, squeezing her shoulder gently.

"I don't know. Maybe? I doubt he would go. He seems content the way he is. I don't think he would want to be fixed, even if there was a way to fix this," she says.

"Mrs. Donaldson was acting weird today, too. She was saying some really uncivil things to me, but she seemed completely oblivious to the fact that she was doing it."

"How odd. You know, I wish none of this ever happened. I don't know how we got these stupid powers, but I wish they would just go away!"

"Speaking of that, Matthew just called me and told me some information he found out. A star that was close to Earth went supernova and blasted everything with radiation.

That's why the power was out and why everyone, well almost everyone, has superpowers."

"Really? That sounds like a science fiction movie or something." She lets out a big sigh. "Things were so great before Philip got his superpowers, and now I'm afraid our marriage is about to end."

She starts crying again.

"Just give it time, Elizabeth. Maybe he will see the error of his ways and be able to change."

"Maybe."

"Why don't you just relax on the couch, and I'll make us some hot chocolate."

"You have a broken leg, Madeline. I should be the one making stuff for you."

"You're my guest. Anyway, I've been getting the hang of maneuvering around, and I want to feel useful."

I go to the kitchen and make the hot chocolate. Carrying both mugs is going to be a bit harder than I thought. Once I am back to the living room, Elizabeth starts to move like she is going to help, but I give her a look to let her know that I'll not be having any of that. She sits back and watches me, looking amused. I manage to hand her the cup without spilling any.

"Thanks," Elizabeth says as she takes her mug. "So, let's talk about something that will take my mind off from what's going on. Anything good happening with you lately?"

"I went on a date last night."

"You did? With who?"

"My neighbor, Ian. He is magnificent," I say with a smile. It feels so good to be able to smile again. These last few weeks have been filled with so many tears and so much anger, I thought I would never smile again.

"Is that the guy you keep mentioning? I don't think I've ever met him before. What's he like? What did you guys do? Come on girl, give me some details!" Elizabeth says, clearly feeling a bit better.

So, I fill her in on my date. The nice meal that I shared with Ian and the not so nice telekinetic man.

"Jeez! Like I said, these powers don't seem like a good thing anymore."

"I agree with you and not just because of my bitterness at not having them," I chuckle.

"So, did Ian show you what his power is, other than being a stud?"

"No, actually, he told me that he doesn't have one either."

"What do you know? Sounds like you two were made for each other," Elizabeth says, smiling warmly.

"It's too early to tell, but I do like him a lot. He even seems to really like me. He practically asked me to go to on a trip to Scotland with him."

Elizabeth almost chokes on her hot chocolate. She starts coughing.

"What?! Don't you think that's a little fast for it being your first date? Are you sure he isn't a stalker?"

"Don't worry. He seemed to pick up on my reservations and apologized right away."

"What did you say?"

"I just smiled and told him we should probably go on another date before doing a trip like that."

"So, are you? Going on another date, I mean."

"Yes, but he hasn't officially asked me out yet."

"Hopefully, he will soon. No time like the present."

We spend the next hour just talking and reminiscing about our childhood. Games we used to play, boys we used to like, teachers we miss and ones we don't. We finally hit a quiet spell, and I ask her if she would like to watch some TV.

The TV is on a channel I was watching a news report on earlier. There's a report on right now, so I stop to see what it's about.

"...*an epidemic of people hospitalized with veins that appear to be glowing blue. Doctors are unsure what the cause is at this point. There have been reports of many patients becoming confused and some even becoming overly aggressive. We have received word that a star close to the earth went supernova and saturated the world with radiation. Scientists are still looking into what that might mean for humanity.*"

"Looks like it isn't just Philip who's going crazy. Sorry, that sounded bad," I apologize quickly, hoping I don't bring on another five minutes of crying. I wouldn't want her to become dehydrated or something.

"Don't worry about it. Even though it's happening to other people, it still doesn't make me feel better. He is the father of my child!"

"What did he say when you told him about the baby?"

"I haven't had the chance to. I've been waiting for the right moment, but it just never seems to present itself. He is either off having an adrenaline rush or he's home yelling at me."

"Maybe if you told him, he would snap out of it and stop yelling at you."

"Yeah, maybe."

Just then the news comes back on after the break.

"*I'm here live from Chicago. As you can see behind me, there's a riot going on. The police have lost all control. It appears that the rioters are using their powers to loot businesses in the area and are retaliating when the police try to gain control. Reports have it that this is not the only city dealing with this kind of criminal activity. In some cities, it has gone as far as murders in the streets."*

Just then a police officer walks by the camera, blood dripping from a huge gash on his lip.

"Hey sir . . . sir . . . could you please come tell us what you know about the current state of things?"

"The current state of things? Can't you see what's going on back there? Things ain't looking good, lady! With the whole world full of superhumans, the police can't catch all the criminals. It seemed like things were fine at first, but now there are freaks with glowing blue veins, acting crazy and starting fights. We're outnumbered!"

Just then he turns to address the camera directly, eyes wild.

"The police department is asking that if anyone has the power of being bullet proof or has super strength or speed, anything useful, would you please come down to the police station and we'll give you training to help us with these criminals."

Suddenly, a group of men with visible glowing veins run past the camera, carrying merchandise they must have just stolen. We see the police officer turn to face them. He blows a gust of air that knocks them down. He starts running over to them, but one of the men holds out his hand and covers the road with a thick layer of ice. The police officer slips and falls, giving the men a chance to stand up and run.

The camera turns back to a slightly hysterical news reporter.

"There you have it, ladies and gentlemen. The world has gone mad! We advise that you stay inside your homes. If there are any people willing to stand up and be brave, the police are asking for volunteers to come to their aid."

I turn off the TV. Elizabeth's expression mirrors how I feel; clearly shaken and afraid. I am so glad I live in a little town. If I lived in a big city, I don't think I would ever want to go outside again. I suppose this sort of thing could happen here too, but it seems less likely.

"Are you okay with me staying here over night? I'm afraid to go home right now, with Philip acting crazy and my house being so close to the city limits."

"Of course. That's what best friends are for."

You would think that we would run out of things to talk about, after spending an entire day together, but that's the great thing about our friendship. We never do. After a while, Elizabeth calls it a night and decides to turn in. Before I head to bed, I double check my front lock, just in case.

In the morning, I get started on making breakfast. Elizabeth helps set the table, but then her cell phone goes off. She steps into the living room to take it. When she comes back, she's shaking.

"Is everything okay, Elizabeth?"

"No! Philip is in the hospital."

CHAPTER EIGHTEEN

VINCENT

"I got it! Wisconsin. She's from Wisconsin," Frank says, stumbling out of the bedroom.

"I know a guy from Wisconsin . . . Barty Jones. He's got quite the arsenal on his property. Enough to arm a small militia. I should give him a call, see if he's got some extras he could part with." Pete says. He walks over to their computer. "I'll search online for a map of Wisconsin."

"There it is," Vincent says, pointing to the screen. "Did you get a location in Wisconsin? Or do we gotta knock on every door in the whole state lookin' for this chick?"

"Umm. Let me think . . ." Frank says, sitting down on the couch. He closes his eyes and rubs his forehead as though he's trying to coax the memory out. Vincent takes notice of what Pete's been worried about. Frank's veins are glowing brightly under his skin. Vincent just shrugs it off and hopes it doesn't mean anything. These visions are the only thing helping them to plan their attack.

"I can see a sign . . . It's a small town."

"Again, not really helpful. Think, Frank. Try to picture that sign. What's it say?" Vincent asks.

"Amherst. It says Amherst," Frank says, jumping to his feet. He walks back over to the computer to see where Amherst is.

"How do you spell that?" Pete asks.

"You're such an idiot. A-m-h-e-r-s-t," Vincent answers.

"There. Right there. Close to the center of the state," Pete says pointing to the screen.

"That's a long way from Texas," Frank comments.

"Are you sure she ain't from Chicago or Milwaukee or somethin'? If she is a scientist who was behind the event, that's no place for a government research facility."

"That's the point of secret research facilities. They would be in unlikely places. So what's the plan?" Vincent asks. "How are we gonna get to Wisconsin? The planes ain't carryin' passengers yet."

"We'll drive. If we take turns driving, we can be there in less than a day," Pete suggests.

"Yeah, sure. If my piece of crap car will make it that far without falling apart. Frank, did you get a look at her? What's she look like?" Vincent asks.

"I don't know. I didn't see her. I can try to sleep in the car. See if I can find out what she looks like."

"Well boys. Get packed and let's go. We finally have our chance to fight back," Vincent says.

CHAPTER NINETEEN

MADELINE

"What happened, Elizabeth?"

"I don't know yet. That was my neighbor. He said that he found Philip outside, lying unconscious in front of our door. He called the ambulance, and they rushed Philip to the hospital. I need to go. Thanks for letting me stay, Madeline."

"Did you want me to come with you?"

"No, that's okay. I'll call you to let you know what's going on."

I give her a hug goodbye and then finish making breakfast. I sit down at the table with a steaming plate of scrambled eggs and toast. I don't have much of an appetite now. After watching the disturbing news last night and now with my best friend's husband being in the hospital, my nerves are making me feel slightly sick. I eat what I can, but scrape the rest into the garbage. Just then, Mrs. Donaldson walks in.

Her appearance causes me to startle. She looks like she is only a couple of years older than me now. Her hair is jet black, her skin is flawless—not a wrinkle to be seen—and she's walking upright and gracefully. The only problem is that her veins are the brightest blue I have ever seen them.

"Mrs. Donaldson! You look . . . amazing!"

"Thanks, Madeline. You look . . . ordinary," she says.

Clearly, she's still not herself. That friendly sparkle in her eye is gone, replaced with a look of petulance. I do not like this change in her.

"Did I just see a car pull out this morning? You have another man on the side?" she asks.

"What? No! That was my best friend, Elizabeth. She stayed over for the night because her husband was scaring her. But then her neighbor called to say that he got sent to the hospital."

"Oh. Well, that is unfortunate."

"Yes. I feel so bad for her. She's going through a rough time."

"No, I wasn't talking about your friend. I meant it was unfortunate that you didn't have a male visitor."

"Mrs. Donaldson! I'm not that way. Besides, I like Ian."

"Yes, well, I think you would make a nice couple."

I look at her to see if she is being sincere, and it appears that she means it. Her eyes look friendly again, instead of a look of annoyance or disdain. I'm having a hard time keeping up with these personality changes.

"Mrs. Donaldson, have you been noticing any mood swings lately?"

"Not really. Why do you ask?"

She looks so completely innocent when she says it, I can't help but believe she knows nothing about what's happening to her. I wish she was the same old lady I used to take care of. I can't stand these outbursts. I may have to ask her to stop coming over. I'll just have to learn to take care of myself.

"Well, um, no reason. I don't have too much for you to do. Maybe you could make the beds, if you don't mind."

"Not at all, dear."

It's so weird hearing the phrases Mrs. Donaldson usually says to me, coming from a twenty-something year old. It appears that her mind hasn't gotten younger.

I decide to try to unload the dishwasher while she goes to the bedrooms. Chores take a lot more effort and time when you only have one useful leg. I take it slow, but suddenly, a glass slips from my hand and shatters on the floor. Mrs. Donaldson races in to the kitchen.

"What are you doing, you foolish girl? Why do I even come over here if you're going to do idiotic things to make more work for me?" she yells furiously.

And I start to cry. I've never been good with people yelling at me, and right now, my heart aches so badly for the sweet Mrs. Donaldson to come back and stay, that I am overcome with grief.

"Wipe away those tears! My God, Madeline. I don't know what Ian sees in you. Lately, you have become a snively, useless, waste of space."

"Get out!" I yell through my tears.

"What?" she responds, anger turning to shock.

"I said, get out!"

"Fine," she says, suddenly looking confused and hurt.

"And don't bother coming back! I don't need your insults! I don't need you!"

Mrs. Donaldson looks like she is about to say something, but turns to leave. Once she closes the door, I break down completely. Everyone in the world has gone mad! Maybe I don't want to live in a world where everyone has superpowers and are becoming complete jerks!

Suddenly, my phone rings. It better not be Mrs. Donaldson. I feel like I don't ever want to talk to her again.

I let it ring a few times, but I just can't stop myself from picking it up.

"Hey, Madeline."

My heart skips a beat. It's Ian. I take a moment to clear my throat and try to act as though I haven't just been crying my eyes out.

"Hi, Ian. How have you been?"

"I've been fine. I was outside and I heard some yelling coming from your direction and then Mrs. Donaldson was walking back to her place, sobbing. Is everything okay?"

"No. No, it's not. Mrs. Donaldson has been changing and not just her appearance. She is downright offensive to me most of the time. I told her to leave and never come back."

"I'm sorry to hear that. I know you thought very fondly of her."

I did."

There's a pause.

"Well, Mrs. Donaldson wasn't the only reason I called."

"Oh?" I say, holding back the sudden wave of excitement. There's another pause before he starts talking again.

"I enjoyed our first date, and I was wondering if you would be willing to go out with me again?"

"I would love to."

"Great! How about this Saturday? I thought maybe a picnic lunch in the park would be nice."

"That sounds wonderful. What would you like me to bring?"

"Nothing. I'll take care of everything."

"Are you sure?"

"Yes. This is my chance to show off my cooking skills."

"Uh-oh! You're not planning on serving me haggis, are you?" I say, teasingly.

"How'd you guess?" he laughs. "I'll pick you up around ten, and we can maybe take a little walk first."

"I hope you don't mind going slow. I'm still not a pro with my crutches yet."

"Not a problem, at all. You can enjoy the sights better when you take your time. Anyway, I should probably go. I look forward to seeing you, Madeline."

"Same here, Ian."

I am just sitting down to read, when I hear a knock at the door. I look to see who's there and it's Mrs. Donaldson again. I want to just ignore her until she takes a hint and goes back home, but she looks a little worried. I decide to let her in.

"What do you want?"

"Oh, Madeline, dear! I am so sorry for the last visit. I clearly upset you."

"Yes, you did."

"I just wish I knew what is going on. Half the time I can't remember what I'm doing or where I'm going. I feel like I'm going crazy. All I remember is you yelling at me to never come back."

I put my arm around her shoulder and my frustration with her melts away as I remember how much I really do care about her.

"You feel warm, Mrs. Donaldson. Are you feeling all right?"

"No, actually, I'm not feeling so well. Help me to a chair, please Mad. . ."

Before I can catch her, she faints. I bend down to feel for a pulse. There is one, but it's weak. Panicking, I pull my cell phone out of my pocket and call an ambulance.

CHAPTER TWENTY

VINCENT

"**F**rank. Frank! Wake up! We're here," Vincent says as they drive past the town sign.

"Think they got a hotel or somethin'?" Pete asks.

"How the hell would I know?" Vincent says with a yawn. Pete and Vincent did all the driving, since Frank was sleeping most of the time. He did wake up at one point and warn them that they were going to run something over that would give them a flat tire and was able to keep it from happening.

They take their time going down Main Street, looking for a place to stay. They see a big Lutheran church, a couple of bars and restaurants, a small hardware store, a bank, a coffee shop, and some other businesses they are unable to identify in the few seconds it takes to drive past.

"There's a gas station," Pete says, pointing straight through the intersection. "Go ask if there's a place to stay in town."

They pull into the station and ask the attendant if there's a hotel nearby.

"There's a bed and breakfast down the street or a motel just on the edge of town."

"Where's the motel?" Vincent asks.

"I didn't take you guys for the B&B types," he says chuckling, eyeing them up. "Go straight through the intersection until you get to the stop sign and take a left. The motel is just a little ways down the road on the right, before you cross over the river. Where you guys from?"

They walk away without answering and get back in the car. They drive back through town and spot the B&B the guy told them about. It's a large mansion that looks like a nice place, except it's pink.

"Pink? Who would paint a huge house like that pink?" Vincent mutters, shaking his head.

The motel is next to a supper club. The sign for the motel is old and weathered, but it states that there is vacancy.

"Looks cheap. Good," Vincent comments. "Frank, for the love of God, wake up!"

"It's getting harder to wake him up," Pete says, worriedly.

"Go get us a room. I'll work on Frank," Vincent says. Pete walks away, searching for the office to rent a room. Vincent climbs in the back seat next to Frank.

"Frank, wake up," he says shaking Frank's shoulder. Frank continues sleeping, his eyes are darting back and forth under his eyelids. Vincent lifts one of Frank's eyelids and sees his hazel eye rolling around in the socket, but he still doesn't wake up.

"Damn it, Frank, wake up!" Vincent says, slapping Frank across the cheek. He grunts, but follows that up with a snore, turning his head the other direction.

"You asked for it," Vincent says, getting frustrated. He zaps Frank's injured shoulder with a small electric shock, hoping the pain will do the trick.

"Ow! Knock it off, you prick!" Frank wakes with a howl, pushing Vincent's hand away. "Dude, you woke me up just as I was dreamin' about her . . . at least, I'm pretty sure it was her."

"Pretty sure? You better know for sure," Vincent says.

"Okay, okay. It was her. First, I saw her in some lab talking with a guy who was wearing a white lab coat. He was really excited about something. Then the dream changed. She was walking on a path in the woods with another guy. . . "

"That's it! See?" Vincent interrupts. "She was in a lab with another scientist. She's gotta be a government scientist that had somethin' to do with the blackout and the powers. What does she look like?"

"Um, she had red hair, green eyes, freckles," Frank says, closing his eyes in concentration. "But most importantly, her leg is broken and she's walking around in a cast."

"That sounds promising. Good work, Frank," Vincent says. Frank beams with pride as Pete comes walking back to the car.

"I got us a room with two queen beds and a sleeper sofa," Pete says, handing Vincent an extra key. They grab their bags and make it to the room.

"Bed," Vincent calls out as he walks in the room.

"Bed," Pete says following Vincent.

"Screw you guys," Frank says, slamming his bag down by the worn-out couch.

"Frank got a good vision of Madeline. By what he described, it ain't gonna be hard to find her. Red hair and a broken leg."

"So what's our plan? We gonna just walk around town carryin' guns and shoot her once we see her?" Frank asks.

"We need a better plan than that. We gotta be more discreet if we wanna get away with it. You never know what powers someone else might have. Frank, you got any other tidbits to give?" Vincent asks.

"Well, I saw her walking with some guy in a park. Other people was there too," Frank says.

"That don't help," Pete starts to say.

"Maybe it does," Vincent says, "If there was a lot of people there, you can probably guess it was on a weekend. Frank, you know where they were?"

"Nope. Just on a trail in the woods," Frank says with a yawn. He flops down on the couch, and watches a big cloud of dust billow up from the cushions and sparkle in the sunlight.

"Don't worry, we'll find her and take her out. And I ain't talkin' about dinner and dancin' either," Vincent says with a laugh. "If she's in Frank's dreams, she's gotta be important. We'll be takin' one government monkey outta the picture."

"I don't know. What if we're wrong? What if she don't work for the government? What if she's just a scientist that finds a way to remove the powers?" Pete says, almost sounding hopeful.

"Dude, what's your problem? I can't tell if you are in on this plan or not," Vincent says, raising his voice.

"I wanna take down the government. I do. I just got this bad feelin' about these powers is all," Pete says, his voice shaking. Just then Frank lets out a loud snore and startles them both.

"He's sleeping again? This ain't right. See what I mean, Vince? Frank can't even stay awake for more than an hour no more," Pete says, his watery eyes darting between Frank and Vincent.

"We came all this way. I ain't backing out now. Whether she works for the government and finds a way to take away

our powers, or had somethin' to do with us gettin' them, it
don't matter once she's dead. Either way, she deserves it! Now,
stop carryin' on like a sissy, and find a map or something that
shows where some parks are around here," Vincent says with
a huff.

Pete walks over to the nightstand by the bed closest to the
bathroom, his rain jacket swishing as he walks. He pulls open
the drawer and finds a bible, a notepad, and a phone book.

"No map. Check the dresser," Pete points towards the low
dresser that an old box television is sitting on.

"Nothin'," Vincent says, after pulling open all four drawers.

"I'll go ask the motel guy," Pete says, heading towards the
door.

"Have at it," Vincent says, dropping onto the hard bed.
Exhaustion wins out and he's asleep in a matter of minutes.

CHAPTER TWENTY-ONE

MADELINE

I stand at the doorway while the paramedics put Mrs. Donaldson into the back of the ambulance. I feel a little guilty for getting so angry at her. It's obvious that it wasn't really *her* saying those mean things to me, but the sickness from the radiation.

Once the ambulance is gone, I hobble to my recliner and flop down. There is so much going on, I feel exhausted. I know I shouldn't, but I decide to turn on the news again. Maybe there have been some positive developments elsewhere in the midst of my chaos.

After about two minutes, I turn it back off. Things are not better. They are decidedly worse. Hospitals, jails, and psychiatric wards are starting to fill up all over the world. People are either getting ill, like Mrs. Donaldson, or losing their minds because of radiation poisoning, or whatever it is they're calling it. People are either becoming criminals or they're going mad. If there isn't a cure soon, I'm afraid all of humanity will be doomed. I take a deep breath and try to put it out of my mind. All I can do is trust that God will take care of it.

I have been checking my "Powerless" Facebook group regularly, too. Nobody has joined. And I can't find any articles online saying there are other people that don't have superpowers, either. It seems like Ian and I are the only ones in the world without the powers.

The rest of the week passes without too much excitement, which is nice for a change. Other than a visit to Mrs. Donaldson in the hospital, I spend a lot of time just reading, doting on my cats, and thinking about my upcoming date with Ian. I also gave Mrs. Yates a call and told her that I would like to come back to work next week, even if it's just for a couple of hours. Maybe once Mrs. Donaldson is out of the hospital, things will start being normal again.

CHAPTER TWENTY-TWO

VINCENT

"You do it. I walked around all day yesterday, and didn't see anyone that looked like her. It's your turn," Vincent says.

"But you can just electrocute her and be done with it," Pete says, once again growing jealous of Vincent's power. He's sick of his own power. He can't even take a shower anymore. The water just soaks into his skin and he stays bloated until he pees it out. He looks at the back of his hands and is greeted with veins glowing brighter than they were a couple of days ago.

"I told ya, I ain't goin' out today," Vincent says getting comfortable on the bed.

"I wish Frank would wake up. It would be nice to know when and where she's gonna be at the park. I didn't see her in town at all. This is harder than we thought," Pete says, giving Frank a concerned glance. Frank hasn't woken up since they made it to the motel, two days ago.

"Stop whining and get going. It's Saturday and it's nice outside. This might be it," Vincent says excitedly.

"I don't know, Vince."

"Look. We're here to stop the government a-holes from getting away with manipulating us again. They gave us these powers and now they wanna take 'em away. If they want to take 'em away, that's a good reason to keep them! If we can take one scientist chick out, and thwart their plans somehow, then we should do it. You could be a hero, man." Vincent encourages.

"You know what? You're right! I'm sick of being told what to do," Pete says, getting some of his fire back. Although," Pete says contemplatively, "if Frank's right and there's lots of people out there, maybe I should take a knife instead of a gun. The gunshot will draw attention and I might get caught."

"Do what you gotta do, man. Just get it done. Then we can figure out our next move." Vincent says.

Pete grabs his large hunting knife and heads out the door, with a new spring in his step.

CHAPTER TWENTY-THREE

MADELINE

Finally, Saturday has arrived. We're going on a picnic, so I dress casual: jeans, a nice purple shirt, and a comfortable walking shoe. After resting all week, my leg feels relatively good. Maybe I will be able to go for a more significant walk. I do love hiking.

There's a knock at my door. He's here. I take a deep breath to settle my heart rate.

"Hi, Ian."

"Hey, are you ready to go?"

"Absolutely. Just let me lock up and we can head out."

Ian takes me to the same park where I did my "superpower" testing. The feeling of anger and fear from that day starts to creep into my mind, but I push those thoughts away and focus on Ian. It really is a beautiful park. There are a number of gorgeous trails that wind their way through the woods. I enjoy walking them alone, so I know I'm going to enjoy them that much more having Ian along. There are a bunch of cars parked here already. Looks like it might be busy today. It's a perfect day for it.

We get started on a trail that is heavily shaded. The light is streaming through the trees, causing the early autumn leaves to glow varying shades of green, yellow, and orange. A slight breeze is blowing, making the shadows dance, and sunlight to shine through the woods like spotlights. It's breathtaking.

"So, how have you been, Madeline?"

"I've been doing all right. I'm so glad to be out of the house. It felt like I was going crazy from sitting around so much."

"We wouldn't want that. I don't want to have to come visit you in an insane asylum," he says, with a slight smirk on his face. "Have you heard any updates on Mrs. Donaldson?"

"Yes. I went and visited her in the hospital. She's stable, but she is not doing great. Her veins are glowing brightly all the time now, and she has some pretty severe mood swings and confusion. I guess she threw something at a nurse the other day," I sigh. "I feel so bad for her. Even though she's young and isn't suffering from arthritis now, I wish she was back to the way she used to be."

We stop walking for a second so that a group of people can walk past us. My crutches take up a lot of space.

"I've only talked with her a few times, but she was always so sweet when we did talk. She was even the one who suggested I take you out on a date. One of the best pieces of advice I have ever received," Ian says, smiling warmly. He sure knows how to make a girl feel special.

After they've passed, we start walking again. I can't help but feel a bit uneasy with all these people around. Perhaps I'm getting too paranoid, but after what I've seen, how do we know we can trust anyone? Everyone seems to have some level of a blue glow in their veins.

"Ian, can I ask you something? Do you feel at all worried about what is going on in the world?"

"I presume you're talking about how everyone seems to have radiation poisoning, superpowers, and crazy blue glowing veins? Of course. There really isn't anything I can do about it, though, so I just kind of ignore it all as much as I can. I know you struggled with not having superpowers for a while, but I have to confess, I'm glad I don't have to worry about you losing your mind and becoming unstable like Mrs. Donaldson."

"Me too. I did feel like I was losing my mind over not having superpowers, but not anymore. You have no idea how much relief it brought me when you told me you didn't have any powers either."

Ian smiles weakly in response.

The path we are on loops back around to the picnic area. I find a table that isn't being used while Ian goes back to the car to get our lunch. I sit back while he sets the table. First, he lays out a red and white checkered cloth. Then he places an actual china plate in front of me with silverware and a cloth napkin. Next, he places the food he prepared between us: bruschetta spread on French bread with a little mozzarella cheese melted on top, a cheese platter with slices of deli meats, a container of crackers, a bowl of grapes, cut up bagels, a kind of dip that tastes so remarkable I have to try hard not to lick the bowl clean once it's gone, and a bottle of wine, complete with two fluted glasses. Simple, yet elegant. For dessert, he pulls out beautifully decorated, chocolate dipped strawberries.

"Did you make these yourself?" I ask in awe.

"Sure. It wasn't that hard. Plus, I wanted to impress you."

"It worked; I am impressed."

We take our time eating and enjoying the beautiful day, as well as the pleasure of each other's company. I help him clean up once we're done.

"How's your leg holding up? Would you like to go for another short walk? I mean, we don't have to since you have crutches and everything . . . "

"I don't mind. I'd love to."

We take another path that is apparently the hot spot for the day. There are a lot of people out here. I keep stepping off to the side to let others pass, to be courteous, but also because I want to put as much distance between me and these people as I can. I'm just starting to straighten back onto the path to walk again, when a man wearing a green rain jacket starts walking right at me. It's beautiful outside. Why is this guy wearing a rain jacket?

Most people have been accommodating and try to walk around me, so I just tuck my crutches in a bit, hoping he can make it past. Suddenly, Ian jumps in front of me and shoves the man away, yelling at him to stop. The man stumbles and falls, dropping a knife. Then he scrambles to pick the knife up and gets back to his feet. He looks as though he's going to try to attack me again, but stops when a crowd of people show up and start staring at him. He suddenly looks nervous, swears, and runs away. I look at Ian just in time to see the blue glow of his veins fade away.

"What just happened? How did you know he had a knife and was about to attack me?"

I start to panic.

"Ian, did I just see your veins glow blue?" I ask, as tears start forming in my eyes.

"Madeline, I can explain," Ian says, with a pleading look in his eyes.

I start to lose it.

"You lied to me! You told me you didn't have any superpowers! How could you?"

I turn and start hobbling away as fast as I can. He catches up to me, which really isn't hard.

"Please, Madeline. Let me explain."

"No! How can I know that what comes out of your mouth won't just be another lie? I knew you were too good to be true."

I feel like my whole world is shattering around me. I was just almost attacked by a lunatic, which is bad enough, but the one person who made me feel special and kept me from feeling alone in this world, lied to me. Deceived me. I let him in. I trusted him, and this is what happens?

"At least let me drive you home, Madeline. I promise, I won't talk until you are ready to hear what I have to say."

I reluctantly oblige and let him take me home, only because I really have no other option. After almost being stabbed, I don't want to spend another second here, and he's the one who drove us. He is true to his word and doesn't speak at all in the car. The look of anguish on his face pulls at my heart a bit, but I am so completely broken, I don't let it affect me.

I make it back into my place and lock the door behind me. That's when the flood of misery hits me. I crumple to the floor and cry. I cry until I cannot cry any more. Somehow, I find myself lying on my bed. I cannot even remember how I got there. My mind is completely numb.

It's starting to get dark when I realize I've been lying in bed, staring at the wall for the last few hours. Only one thought keeps running through my mind.

I am alone.

I am truly alone in this cursed world. It is only a matter of time before all of humanity falls prey to the radiation illness. My parents, Matthew, Elizabeth, and now Ian. I'm not sure how he was able to keep this secret. I didn't even see his veins glow before today. I am so mad at Ian, that I push any thoughts I have about him down and bury it under my self-loathing and misery.

I must have fallen asleep at some point because I startle awake after having a terrible nightmare. In my dream, I was standing in a field. The breeze was blowing, moving heavy clouds in front of the sun. The bodies of everyone I love and know were laying at my feet, dead. The blueness of their veins seemed to have seeped into their eyes, turning them completely blue. Their eyes stare, unseeing, towards the cloudy sky. And I knew it was only a matter of time before I would be dead as well.

CHAPTER TWENTY-FOUR

VINCENT

"What're you doin' back? The day ain't over yet," Vincent says, as Pete walks back into the motel room.

"I found her," Pete says, looking down at his feet.

"And? Did you do it?" Vincent asks, sitting up on the bed.

"No. I saw her walking down the trail with her crutches. I got excited and was heading straight towards her with my knife drawn, but her boyfriend stepped in front of her and pushed me down. I picked the knife back up and was gonna finish the job, even if I had to kill him too, but a bunch of people started gatherin'. It was too damn busy! I got freaked out and ran."

"You could've waited around to get her. This was your chance and you blew it!" Vincent says, getting angry.

"Sorry. I saw all them peoples standing around, and I started wonderin' what would happen if they attacked me. I don't know what kinda powers they got. They coulda killed me, so I ran."

"Well, at least you coulda died for a good cause. I'm so sick of you being a little pansy! You talk and talk about fightin' against the government, and yet you can't handle killin' one girl. I swear, you've become more and more of a lily liver since we got these powers. I want revenge for what they did to my Maggie!" Vincent yells as sparks start shooting out of his fingertips. He stands up seething and starts walking towards Pete, glaring at him. Pete takes a few steps backwards looking scared.

"We'll get her. We will. This is a small town. We'll find her again, Vince," Pete says, backing up against the front door holding his hands out in front of him. Before Vincent stops to think about it, he shoots Pete with an electric current, wanting to hurt him to channel some of his anger. Pete drops to the floor convulsing, as though being tasered. He stops abruptly and Vincent looks with horror at Pete's smoking body. He drops to the floor next to him.

"Pete? Pete! I only wanted to zap you, Petey. Wake up," Vincent says, patting Pete on his pockmarked face. He feels for a pulse. Pete's dead.

"What have I done!?"

He shoots another smaller electric current into Pete's chest, over his heart. He checks for a pulse. Nothing. He tries again, and again. He finally gives up and lays his head on Pete's chest, weeping from the guilt of having just murdered his friend. After a while, he stands up and walks over to Frank to wake him up. Frank just keeps sleeping no matter what Vincent does. He sits down on his bed, thinking about what he should do. He's gotta get rid of Pete's body.

CHAPTER TWENTY-FIVE

MADELINE

The sun's up again, so I manage to bathe, dress, and even choke some food down before retreating to my recliner in the living room. The tears keep flowing; a steady stream that blurs my vision of the wall across the room. Midnight and Euphrates keep me company. They seem to know something is amiss and nuzzle their way onto my lap, trying their hardest to comfort me. It's weird. It seems as though the radiation had no effect on animals what-so-ever. I suppose that's actually a good thing. The last thing we need is animals with strange powers.

My cell phone keeps on ringing, but I refuse to answer it. After the third time of checking it and finding Ian's number displayed, I decided it wasn't worth my time to even check it anymore. I contemplate shutting it off, but that would take effort.

My half-dazed mind keeps drifting to thoughts of everyone in the world losing their minds and having a full-blown zombie apocalypse. Only these zombies are imbued with superpowers and I wouldn't stand a chance against them.

The phone just keeps on ringing, so I decide to check it once more to see who is calling. This time it's my mom.

"Hello?"

"Hey, Goose. How was your date?"

A fresh flood of tears breaks through, and I struggle to take a breath.

"What's the matter? Goose! What happened?"

I find my composure and explain my date, leaving out the part of almost getting stabbed. That's the last thing my mother needs to hear.

"Oh, dear. Oh, I am so sorry, honey. I wish I could make it all better."

"I knew there was a reason I kept myself from dating. I was perfectly happy before I allowed him in. Now I feel lonelier than I have ever felt before."

"Give it time, Madeline. From the things you told me about him, he seems like a nice guy. You might want to give him a chance to explain himself before writing him off completely."

"Maybe, but I don't know how I will ever trust him again. He took advantage of me when I was most vulnerable and lied to me. I don't know how to come back from that."

After drawn out silences and nothing but depressed responses from me, my mom apparently decides to give up any hope of making me feel better. She suggests that I go visit Mrs. Donaldson again, to put some focus on someone else. Maybe by trying to cheer someone else up, I'll be able to snap out of the mood. I grunt in response. She just sighs and promises that she will call soon.

Maybe she's right. Maybe I will try to go visit Mrs. Donaldson.

I don't stay for long. Mrs. Donaldson barely even seems to realize I'm even here. She is clearly not right in the head. She starts mumbling something about a leprechaun living on her eyebrow before she falls asleep. I squeeze her hand once more before I leave.

I ask the nurse if there's any way they can call me if anything happens to Mrs. Donaldson. She tells me that they usually call the closest family member, but since her family lives so far away and has shown no signs of coming to visit her, she will keep my number on hand and call me with any changes. I know that what she is offering is against protocol, so I give her my thanks.

I keep a close eye on every person I pass as I'm leaving. I feel like the hospital is probably one of the safest places there is right now, but even the doctors are showing signs of the radiation poison under their skin.

I get home and lock myself in again. The combination of fresh air and doing something outside of the house helped a bit, but I'm still feeling down in the dumps.

I spend the next day or so doing just enough to keep myself alive. I do go to the library and work a short two-hour shift, just to see how things go. I think the omni-linguism superpower Mrs. Yates has is really starting to addle her brain. I don't think she even realizes when she's speaking a different language, anymore. I decide to just nod my head at her as she chats away in what sounds like Elvish.

There are very few people who show up while I'm working. Mrs. Yates tells me she has seen a major decrease in library patrons. Comic books seem to be the only books being checked out right now. The whole town seems too preoccupied with using their powers and seeing what they can do, that they don't have time to read.

When I get home, I see a small glass vase filled with violets and white roses at my door. They are so beautiful. A handwritten card has been attached with a purple ribbon. I wait until I'm inside to read it.

CHAPTER TWENTY-FIVE

Madeline,

I cannot begin to describe to you the remorse I feel for having deceived you. You deserve so much better than that. I would love to explain to you why I did what I did, but not in a letter. I will wait for you to decide when the time is right to speak, but I will understand if you never want to speak to me again. Just know this, you were the shining light in my otherwise gray world. I long to see you again. Please, Madeline, give me a chance to explain.

Ian

I have to admit, this letter makes me want to run over to his house and forgive him, but the fact that he lied to me floods my mind again, and I grow angry and hurt once more. I'm not ready to talk to him.

I set the flowers on my end table and slip the card into the drawer. I don't want to throw it away . . . not just yet.

I stick to my books most of the time now, because the news has become extremely disturbing as of late. The news casters have started rambling off topic while on camera, no longer able to stay focused. A news reporter, apparently with the ability to become invisible, kept disappearing on camera time and time again. You couldn't see her, but you could hear giggling. The camera man finally swore and just shut the camera off. There have also been non-stop news reports about the activities and antics of the crazed population. The last report I watched was of a little old lady commanding a flock of squirrels to attack anyone and everyone in sight, laughing maniacally. I just can't watch anymore.

I am constantly worried about my family. They keep reassuring me that they feel fine, but I know it won't be long before they are affected. They have the blue glow in their veins. I really don't want to be alone in this world of mad, crazy people. Maybe I should consider stocking up on guns and ammunition. I don't like guns, but I'm not sure what else to do. I don't have superpowers to rely on, so I have to protect myself somehow.

Just then the phone rings. A part of me hopes it's Ian, but another part of me wants to stay mad at him forever.

The caller ID says it's Elizabeth.

I can hear her sobbing before I even say anything. Great, Philip must have been released from the hospital and did something terrible again. I sigh.

"Hello?"

I hear Elizabeth's voice squeak as she tries to say something. Whatever it is, it must be bad.

"Elizabeth? What's the matter?"

"He's dead . . . Philip is dead!"

CHAPTER TWENTY-SIX

VINCENT

Vincent walks back into the motel room covered in dirt. He just finished burying Pete's body in the woods behind the motel. Someone had left a shovel sitting out by the office, so he swiped it and dug a grave for Pete.

Things are getting' outta hand. I can't control my anger no more and now I've killed my friend because of it . . . You know what? It's not my fault. It's the damn government's fault. They did this to us and they're gonna pay for it!

He grabs a clean change of clothes and goes to take a shower. Once he undresses, he looks at himself in the cracked mirror; well defined muscles covered in tattoos, scars where he's been cut from knife fights, and veins that are pulsing with a blue glow. *My veins are so bright now. What the hell is causing this?*

He hops in the shower and starts to wash off. He closes his eyes and puts his face in the warm stream of water, rinsing away the sweat and grime. Without warning, Pete's face flashes in his mind's eye. His mouth is slack and his eyes are completely white and lifeless. Then he blinks and looks directly at Vincent.

"You did this to me. You killed me, Vince." Pete accuses.

Vincent quickly opens his eyes, breathing heavily. He finishes up and steps out of the shower. He sees a rat scurrying in the corner of the bathroom, which hasn't been unusual in this God-forsaken place. Vincent grabs his towel and dries his face. He pulls the towel off and he sees the rat standing up on its hind legs, its beady black eyes looking directly at Vincent.

"Shoo! Get outta here!" Vincent yells.

"You killed me, Vince. It's all your fault." The rat says in Pete's voice.

Vincent drops the towel on floor and backs up, horrified.

"No . . . no! This ain't real! Pete's dead. Scram rat!" Vincent yells with a shaky voice.

"You'll get what's comin' to ya . . . " Vincent hears the rat say as it runs away back into a hole in the wall.

I must be exhausted. That couldn't have been real. Vincent chuckles nervously to himself, but he keeps his eyes on the hole as he quickly gets dressed. The rat doesn't come out again. He walks back out to the main room and sees Frank lying on the couch.

"How's it going there, Frankie? Hope you're doin' better than me. Wish I could talk to ya right now. I'm kinda freakin' out a bit here."

He sits down on the bed rubbing his eyes. He's feeling abnormally exhausted for not having done much all day. The old, box TV is as good as broken. It picks up all of one station, a cartoon station, and even that's fuzzy. He lays down and soon he's asleep.

A little girl with long dark hair runs in front of Vincent, giggling sweetly. Her blue dress bounces at her knees as she takes each step. She continues running, weaving through the trees and jumping over fallen branches. The dying light of the day casts long shadows throughout the woods.

"I'm gonna get you, Maggie!" Vincent says, laughing along with her giggles.

Vincent keeps chasing her, smiling so big. Maggie runs ahead, always just out of reach.

"Catch me, Daddy!" She yells, dodging behind a copse of trees.

"Slow down, baby! Be careful!" Vincent says, smile fading as he loses sight of her. He hears her giggle a ways ahead of him. The sunlight is fading fast, making it hard to see.

"Maggie? Where are you, baby?" Vincent calls out, zig zagging between trees.

He hears a small scream in the distance and a faint splash of water.

"Maggie! Maggie, you all right?" He yells, quickening his pace. He hears no response.

He starts to run, branches scratching his face and grabbing at his clothes. He trips and falls over a large tree root, cutting his hands on sharp rocks as he catches himself. He stands back up and makes it deeper in the woods. He can smell the stagnant water before he can see it. He comes up over a small hill and sees a pond down at its base. Maggie's body is floating face down in the algae covered water.

"Maggie . . . Maggie!" Vincent screams out, stumbling down the hill. He runs out into the mucky pond, the cold water rising above his knees. He grabs Maggie and turns her over and reflexively lets go, horrified. Her once baby blue eyes are now glazed over and lifeless, as though replaced with little white marbles. Her gray skin is wrinkled and ice cold to the touch. She appears as though she has been dead for a couple of hours.

Vincent is woken up to screams, but they are not his own. He looks over at Frank and sees that his eyes are wide open staring at nothing and yet seem fixated on something. He's screaming so loudly, Vincent covers his ears and makes his way over to the couch. He has a hard time getting close by him. Frank is thrashing so violently, Vincent worries he might hurt himself.

"Frank, calm down, man! What did you see? What is it?"

Frank keeps screaming, taking short gasps of air. His face is turning bright red and the whites of his eyes start looking unusually blue.

"Shut up, man! Someone's gonna hear you!" Vincent says, panicking. He tries to hold Frank's shoulders down, to keep him still. Frank keeps screaming, his body convulsing under Vincent's hands.

"Shut it!" Vincent says, slapping Frank across the cheek. Frank stops. He stops screaming. He stops convulsing. He stops breathing.

He's dead.

His entire eyes are blue and so wide, they're almost bulging out of their sockets.

"No, no, no! Don't do this to me! You can't leave me! Don't die, Frankie! Wake up, you son of a . . . " Vincent says, pounding on his chest. He continues pounding on Frank's chest until he's dripping with sweat and can't lift his arms anymore. He finally gives up and sits on the edge of his bed, shaking.

I'm losing it. This can't be happening. This has to be a dream. Yes. It's all a dream. I just need to wake up.

Vincent slaps himself hard against his cheek. The stinging on his face helps him to realize he's most definitely awake.

"No! No, this can't be real. Everyone is dead!" Vincent yells, tears springing to his eyes. "I'm going to kill them. Every last one of them. I'm going to kill them all! They took everything from me!" Vincent yells, streaks of lightning flying from his fingers. He is so full of rage, he starts seeing red.

He lets out a gut-wrenching yell until he runs out of air and passes out on the bed.

CHAPTER TWENTY-SEVEN

MADELINE

"What!? How?"

"He was in a coma the whole time he was in the hospital, but then he suddenly woke up, screaming and swearing, completely out of his mind," Elizabeth manages to say between her sobs. "He was thrashing around so much it looked like he was having a seizure, and then his heart just stopped. He's gone! Oh God, Madeline! I don't know what to do!" She starts crying harder.

"You can come stay with me for a while if you want. I could use the company," I say, once she quiets down.

"Are you sure? I don't want to be alone, but I don't want to be a bother, either," Elizabeth sniffles.

"Absolutely. I need a friend right now, anyway."

Elizabeth shows up a couple of hours later with an overnight bag. I do my best to be there for her and push my problems out of my mind. I just hug her and let her cry it out. I cry with her. I can't believe this is happening. Her baby will grow up not having a father.

Then it hits me. I'm not sure how long it will be before Elizabeth starts getting sick. I wonder what the radiation poison running through her system is doing to the baby. I take a look at her arms. Her veins are glowing, but only slightly.

Perhaps, a miracle will happen and Elizabeth and the baby will survive this. I close my eyes and say a desperate prayer.

Elizabeth doesn't talk much for a while. I let her sit in silence and grieve. I can't even fathom the pain she must be feeling. I try to comfort her, but I'm not sure what to say. I slip away to the kitchen and decide to make us a nice meal. I don't know if she will be up for eating anything, but I want to give her a moment to be alone yet still be close by.

She eats a small portion, and once we settle back down in the living room, she starts talking.

"Madeline, I don't know what I am going to do. I don't know how to raise a baby, and now I'm all alone. I can't do this!" she says, borderline hysterical.

"Yes, you can Elizabeth. You're going to be a great mother. You have your family, Philip's family, me, and even my parents to help you if you need it. You are not alone," I say, trying to comfort her.

"Do I? Do I really have everyone to rely on? How long before we all get sick and die like Philip. I am so scared! I'm not even sure if my baby is okay," Elizabeth says, still crying.

"When do you have a doctor's appointment?"

"The hospitals are so busy with the sickness, I haven't scheduled an appointment yet."

"I think you should try to schedule one. Just to ease your mind. I can even come with you, if you would like me to."

"We'll see. Thank you so much for being here for me."

"It's no problem at all." I hesitate, not sure if I should tell her about my problems yet. She doesn't seem to be saying much, so I go ahead. "I'm actually glad that you're here. Things did not go well on my last date with Ian," I say with tears forming in my eyes.

"Oh no, what happened?"

"I was almost attacked by a crazy person, but Ian somehow knew the guy was going to attack me with a knife and stopped it from happening. That's when I caught his veins glowing blue before it faded away. He lied to me! He made me believe he didn't have any powers, but he does," I say, getting angry again.

"You were almost stabbed? God, Madeline, that's scary!" Elizabeth says, looking shocked. "I'm sorry Ian lied to you. He should have been up front with you from the start with the whole powers thing, but I don't think you should hate him. He tried to protect you."

"But he lied to me! I will not tolerate lying, especially in a relationship."

"I'm not saying you shouldn't be upset, but maybe you should give him a chance to explain himself."

"That's what Mom said," I sigh. "You're right. I should probably let him try to explain himself. I am just so angry."

"Understandable. If you don't mind me asking, how was your date before you were almost stabbed?"

"It was actually quite fantastic. He brought a picnic lunch that he prepared himself. He even made chocolate dipped strawberries for me."

"Really? Forget about maybe giving Ian a chance, Madeline, you *need* to give that man another chance," she says with a small smile.

It is nice to see her smile in the midst of this all. I'm going to do everything I can to help her through this. This isn't the first time we've been there for each other. Elizabeth dated quite a bit in high school. Every break-up she had would result in hours of tears and conversation. We would usually meet at one of our houses and spend the evening talking about the recent reject, bingeing on junk food, and then staying up until the wee hours of the morning playing video games or watching movies. Other than the pain of the break-up, it was pretty fun.

Just then the phone rings, piercing the calm silence in our conversation. I don't recognize the number.

"Hello?"

"Is Ms. Hayes there?"

"Yeah, it's me."

"Hi. This is Nurse Kelly from St. Michael's hospital."

"Oh, yes. Hi."

"I am so sorry to say this, but Mrs. Donaldson passed away today."

"What?!"

"I was told that she slipped into a coma last night, and when I came in for my shift today, she had a seizure and then her heart just stopped. I'm so sorry."

I'm in shock, but I manage to slip out a thank you before hanging up.

Not Mrs. Donaldson. Oh please, not Mrs. Donaldson. I feel myself spiraling down into the black abyss that is my mental state. My emotions are so raw from the constant wounds that have been inflicted upon them, I feel I may scream from the anguish.

"Madeline! Hey . . . Madeline!" Elizabeth is calling out, snapping her fingers in front of my face.

I lift my head and try to focus my tear-blurred eyes on her.

"What's happening?"

She looks terrified. I should probably respond.

"Mrs. Donaldson is dead."

Elizabeth sinks onto the couch next to me and we both cry at our losses. I have to be dreaming. This all must be some kind of sick, twisted dream. I want to wake up now.

It's only Elizabeth's presence that's keeping me held together. We spend a lot of time crying, but at least we have one another to share our feelings with. Someone who understands. I know she has it worse, since it was her husband that passed, but all the pain and loss has added up to be too much. I cannot handle much more.

The next day, Elizabeth gets a call from her parents reminding her that she has funeral arrangements to plan. She reluctantly leaves, promising that she will come visit with me soon. I just hope she holds up through all of this.

Time seems to come to a standstill. I just can't make myself care about anything right now. It isn't until I hear pounding on my door and my father's voice calling out my name that I snap to. How long have I been sitting here?

I unlock the door and let him in. He wraps his arms around me and holds me close. I feel my body release tension, just for a moment, and let my dad take care of his little girl. He helps me back to the living room.

"Madeline, I heard about Mrs. Donaldson, and Philip, and what happened on your date."

"How did you hear about all of that?"

"Well, your mother had already told me about your date, but Elizabeth called because she was worried about you, and she let us know what has been going on."

"That was nice of her. She seems to be holding up pretty well, considering."

"You should have called us."

"Sorry. I'm not thinking straight right now. I'm having a hard time dealing with everything."

"I know. That's why I'm here. I decided to come over to heal your leg. It was unfair of me to leave you in pain. I'm sorry I caused more stress on you."

"I understand why you did what you felt you had to do. You were probably right about me. If you had fixed my leg right away, I probably would have kept trying to find what my ability is, expecting you to fix me after getting hurt."

"Are you over that now? You're not going to try something silly again after I fix you, correct?"

"No, Dad. I've come to realize that I don't have any special power, nor do I want one, to be honest. I don't know if you noticed, but the world has gone crazy out there."

"Oh, we noticed. That's why your mom decided to stay home. She doesn't feel safe outside anymore."

"I'm feeling a bit like that right now, too."

"So, are you ready? I really haven't used my power much since I healed your ribs. Only for cuts and bruises."

"Yeah, I'm ready. Thank you for doing this."

My dad kneels and places his hands around my broken leg. I see a sheen of sweat start building on his forehead as he focuses. The pain in my leg turns to an intense itching and then it is gone.

Sweet relief.

I watched my dad while he was healing me. The blue hue he had under his skin grew to an intensity that was hard to even look at. I keep watching, expecting it to go back to being only a little noticeable, but it stays very noticeable. I would say, it looks to be close to the brightness of Mrs. Donaldson's veins the last time she visited me.

My dad stands up, but then quickly sits on the couch next to me. He is breathing hard and his eyes are squeezed shut.

"Dad, are you okay? Your veins are still glowing."

"Just give me a moment."

I rub his back while he recovers. He finally raises his head and takes a deep breath.

"Well, how does it feel?" he asks.

"Amazing! Thank you so much."

He squeezes my shoulder. "You are most welcome."

"Dad, do your veins stay this bright for this long after you heal someone?"

"No. I've never seen them get this bright before," he said, giving the back of his hands a curious look.

Great, I just did something bad to my father! I start to panic a bit.

"I'll be okay, Madeline. I feel just fine," he reassures me. "Well, what are you waiting for? Test out your leg. See if I did a good enough job."

I remove my cast, stand up, and walk pain free around my living room. I even do a couple of jumping jacks. My dad has a big smile on his face as he watches me move around again. I run over to him and give him a big hug.

"Thank you so much! This definitely takes a weight off my mind. Now, if there's a zombie apocalypse, at least I can run."

"A zombie what?" my dad asks, giving me a weird look.

"Never mind."

"Well, I should probably get back to your mother. I wouldn't want her to worry herself to death."

"Uh, yes. That would be terrible." Sometimes my dad's jokes are rather tasteless.

"Are you going to be okay? You could always come along and stay with your mother and me for a while."

"I'll be fine, Dad. I'm feeling a bit more positive now. I might even give Ian a call."

"Good."

I walk him to the door. He kisses me on the forehead and heads out to his car. I haven't stopped smiling since my dad healed my leg, but now my smile fades as I watch my father walk away. The blue glow in his veins fills me with dread.

CHAPTER TWENTY-EIGHT

VINCENT

"**W**here am I?" Vincent wakes up, eyes blurry. He pushes himself up. His head swims and starts pounding. He holds his forehead and squeezes his eyes shut.

"Better question, who am I?" Vincent speaks out loud to no one in particular. He sits at the edge of the bed, trying hard to piece together what's going on. He can't seem to remember his name. The pounding in his head starts to settle down and he opens his eyes to look around at his surroundings. Maybe he can find a clue to point him in the right direction. He catches sight of Frank and gasps.

What the hell?

He stands up and walks towards Frank's lifeless body. The memories of what happened seep back into his mind and he falls to his knees, sobbing. He continues crying for his friends and his little girl until he runs out of tears. He sits on the dirty carpet, leaning against the couch Frank is laying on, staring at a giant crack in the mustard yellow wall across the room. The sun is beginning to go down when Vincent snaps out of his stupor. He stands up and walks to the refrigerator to grab a beer.

What am I gonna do with Frank's body? I guess I could bury him out back by Pete.

He takes a big swig of his beer and sets it down on top of the TV. He makes his way back over to Frank and grabs his legs to see if he can drag him. He tugs hard, but Frank hardly even budges. He pulls with all his might and only manages to slide the couch an inch or so.

"I can't do it. He weighs too much," Vincent says, wiping sweat from his brow. He walks back over to his beer to take another drink.

"It's your fault, Vinny. You killed Pete and now you let me die too," Vincent hears. He whips around to look at Frank. Frank's mouth is gaping open, but unmoving. His blue eyes continuing to stare up at the ceiling.

"Who said that?" Vincent asks, looking around the room. He sees no one. He puts the beer bottle back up to his lips, hand shaking.

"It's your fault Maggie died too. You shoulda been there for her."

"Shut up! Shut up! I don't know what kind of sick joke this is, but you need to show yourself!" Vincent yells.

Nothing.

He slams the beer bottle down and storms out of the motel room. It's almost completely dark now. He makes his way over to the restaurant that's next to the motel. He checks his pockets and finds a small amount of cash. He decides to have something a little more substantial for supper than the junk he has in the motel room.

Maybe my hunger is making me imagine things.

He steps into the restaurant and can smell the delicious aroma of deep fried food and burgers. He walks past the bar, glancing at the other costumers, and stops short. Pete and Frank are sitting at the bar, staring at Vincent with their dead eyes. Vincent closes his own eyes and shakes his head. He opens them again and sees two men sitting in the same place that Pete and Frank were just sitting. A tall skinny guy, wearing an Amherst Falcons baseball cap is looking at Vincent strangely. His fat buddy, smiles and gives an awkward wave toward Vincent.

"What can I get you, sugar?" an attractive waitress asks, walking towards Vincent. He turns his back on the two men.

"I'd like somethin' to eat," Vincent replies.

"Sure. This way," the waitress says, grabbing a menu for Vincent. She leads the way to a table in an empty room.

"Can I get you something to drink?"

"Just water, thanks." He watches as she walks away, eyeing her backside.

Oh man. What am I gonna do? I can't stay in the room with a dead guy. I gotta find somewhere else to stay.

"Here you go, honey. What can I get you?" The waitress asks, batting her long lashes at Vincent, flirtatiously.

"I'll start with a burger and cheese curds and then maybe your phone number once I'm done," Vincent says, eyes running up and down her body slowly.

She chuckles. "We'll start with the burger and cheese curds," she says, giving him a wink.

"Would you care to join me for supper, at least? This place looks kinda dead right now and I could use some company."

She stands still for a moment, eyebrows scrunched in thought, staring at Vincent.

"Sure. I was going on break soon anyway," she says, taking his order back to the kitchen.

CHAPTER TWENTY-EIGHT

You still got it. Maybe I'll have a place to stay tonight, after all.

She walks back to the table and sits across from him.

"The names Dani. Short for Danielle. What's yours?"

Shoot! Should I give her my real name? Eh, might as well. I won't mind her screaming it out later.

"Vincent. My name's Vincent," he says, relieved that he remembered it.

"Well, Vincent, what brings you here? You're staying in the motel, right?"

"Yeah. How'd you know that?" Vincent asks, suddenly suspicious.

"Small town, remember? Word travels fast when there isn't much else to talk about. Where're your friends? I heard you were staying with a couple of guys."

"Oh, they're . . . sleeping. Late night last night. Hey, I was wondering if you happen to know someone in town named, Madeline. We came here to visit her. My friend, Pete, went to school with her and he'd like to see her again," Vincent says, coming up with a lie fast.

"I know there's a girl that works at the library named Madeline. Maybe she's the one you're looking for."

"The library? Hmm . . . I think the girl we're lookin' for is a scientist or somethin'." Vincent says confused. Just then, a waiter brings out their food. Vincent's mouth starts watering at the sight of it.

"A scientist? I don't think we have any scientists in this town," Dani says, picking up a fry from her plate and nibbling on it. "Where are you from? Your accent tells me you aren't from Wisconsin."

"Texas."

Crap! Why don't you just tell her your whole life's story, Vincent! . . . God, her eyes are so beautiful . . .

"Wow! That's a long way to come see a girl. She must be someone real special to make that kind of trip."

"Oh, she is," Vincent says, but then changes the subject so he doesn't give anything else away. "So, what's a gorgeous woman like yourself doing in such a small town? You should be a model or an actress or something with that pretty face of yours."

She laughs. "Nah. I grew up here. I could never think about leaving. All my friends and family are here. And now your friends are here too and ain't never leavin'. Murderer."

Vincent looks up from his supper at her smiling face. "What did you say?"

"I asked if you like it here. It's not much, but it'll grow on you."

Oh man, not again. Get ahold of yourself, Vincent.

"Um . . . yeah. Sure. This place definitely has its perks," he says, winking at her.

"You are one sweet talker. Is that your power? Sweet talking?" She asks with a smirk.

"Why, is it working?"

"Maybe," She pauses, eyeing Vincent up. "I have the power to change my appearance. See, watch," she says, changing her dark brown hair to a bleach blonde color and then back again. "I don't really do it much though. I have no reason to. I like me just the way I am."

"I like you the way you are too."

"You want to see more of me?" She says, getting a mischievous twinkle in her gray eyes.

"Hell, yes, I would," Vincent says.

"Wait here a minute. I'll go see if I can sneak out early." She slips out of the booth and walks to the kitchen. A moment later she comes back, smiling big. "Let's go, sugar."

~~~~~~~~~~

Dani lays on the bed sleeping next to Vincent. He takes a look around the room in the soft lamplight. A huge improvement compared to the motel room, and the company is loads better, too. He lays back with his hands under his head on the soft pillow and starts coming up with a plan for tomorrow.

I need to get my bag out of the motel and then make a little visit to the library. If it's the Madeline that Frank was talking about, I can end all this and go home. But why the hell would she work in a library, though? I bet it's her cover. Wouldn't want to let on that you're a secret government scientist. Vincent thinks, sighing. *Crap! If they find Madeline dead, and I'm missing, Dani is going to tell the police that I was lookin' for her. They would search the motel room and find Frank dead too. I'm never going to get away with this! I'm such an idiot!*

He gets out of bed and gets dressed. He starts pacing across the room. His plan would have worked, had he not bedded a local.

No one else in town knows my name. Pete's the one who paid for the motel room. Maybe I'm over reacting. Maybe she won't make the connection.

He can hear her stirring in the bed.

"Vincent? What is it?" He hears her ask.

He turns around to look at her and lets out a scream. Her face is no longer the beautiful face of the waitress, but of a dirty, pale corpse with solid white eyes. Pete's face. Vincent stumbles backwards and runs into the wall.

"What's gotten into you?"

Her sweet voice coming from Pete's dead face is enough to make Vincent almost throw up. He runs out of the house as fast as he can. Once outside, he keeps running until the catch in his side makes him stop. He puts his hands on his knees, gasping for air. The full moon gives an eerie glow to everything around him.

What the hell is going on with me? I can't take any more of this! I gotta get out of this place.

He makes his way across town, back to the motel. *I gotta get my stuff and find somewhere to stay.* He walks back into the motel room and keeps his eyes averted from Frank's dead body. He throws all his clothes, the pictures of Maggie, and the rest of the food into his duffle bag.

It's only a matter of time before they find Frank's body; I need to get the hell outta here.

He scans the room for the car keys and spots them on the end table next to the couch. He cautiously steps over to the table and reaches for the keys. All-of-a-sudden, Frank's cold hand grabs Vincent's wrist.

"You're gonna die, Vincent. Just like me."

Vincent frantically rips at Frank's fingers to get him to let go. Filled with unbridled fear, he shoots a lightning bolt at Frank's forehead. Once free, he takes a couple of steps back and sees that Frank's body is in exactly the same position it was in before, but now has a smoldering hole between his eyes.

This isn't real. Nope. I must be hallucinating; this can't be real.

Vincent hurries to the door.

CHAPTER TWENTY-NINE

MADELINE

I wake up screaming from another nightmare. A mob of blue-veined, crazed zombies were chasing me through the town, wanting nothing more than to devour my flesh and make me one of their legion. At the front of the mob was my father. The love he usually holds in his eyes when he looks at me, was replaced by pure hatred. He wanted me dead, and he wanted it to be by his hands.

It takes me a lot less time to get myself ready for the day. I take great relish in moving around my duplex crutch free. I'm going to invite Ian over to talk today. I feel I at least owe him that much. He did save my life.

As I'm cleaning up my place, a fresh wave of grief hits me as I remember that it wasn't that long ago that Mrs. Donaldson was here doing this for me. Poor Mrs. Donaldson.

Once I feel like my place is tidy enough for visitors, I grab my phone and call Ian.

He answers after only one ring.

"Madeline?"

"We need to talk. Could you please come over when you have a chance?" I say, keeping my voice as even as I can.

"I'll be right there," he says sounding eager.

It only takes five minutes before my door bell is ringing.

"Please come in, Ian."

He walks past me and the smell of his cologne almost makes me lose my resolve.

No. I'm still angry at him for lying. I will not be weak just because he looks and smells amazing. Wow, I never noticed that cute line of freckles across his nose before. *Stop it brain!*

He sits on my couch, but I choose to not sit next to him. I sit in my recliner instead.

"Your leg. You don't have a cast on. How?" Ian asks with a look of surprise.

"My dad visited me yesterday. He decided to heal me since I'm dealing with a lot of bad things right now."

Ian looks down at the floor. I can see he feels bad. Good. He should.

"Did you hear about Mrs. Donaldson?" I ask. It may be petty of me, but I want him to know all about the hurtful things I've been dealing with, on top of his deception.

"No. What happened?"

"She died," I say and then I start crying. Maybe it wasn't a good idea. The hurt is still too near. "So did my best friend's husband."

"Oh, Madeline. I am so sorry," he says, tears starting to form in his eyes, too, and if I'm not mistaken, his veins look just a little bit brighter.

I take a breath and gather myself again.

"Well, as you can now see, my dad felt that I had too many horrible things happening to me as of late. It turns out that having my leg healed gave me a clearer head to be able to deal with my emotional pain, now that I don't have to deal with the physical pain." I clear my throat and try to control my emotions. "So I decided to talk with you. Let's hear it. Why did you lie to me, Ian?"

He takes a deep breath and looks at me with great sadness in his gorgeous hazel eyes.

"First off, I just want to say that I am so incredibly sorry, Madeline. I should have told you the truth from the beginning."

I just nod my head at him and say nothing, waiting for him to continue.

"I have the ability to feel other peoples' emotions. I can feel what they feel. If it's intense enough, it starts to consume my mind," he takes another deep breath. "When I visited with you the first time, after your leg was broken, I could feel the loneliness and sadness you were feeling. It broke my heart. I wanted nothing more than to be able to fix it. So, I lied. I made the rash decision to try to make things all better as soon as possible, and so I told you that you weren't the only one without powers. I knew that would make your feelings of loneliness go away. And it worked. You suddenly started feeling hope and happiness. I felt guilty for lying to you, but I was so relieved that you were feeling happy again."

"Whether you thought you were helping me or not, it was still wrong for you to lie to me, Ian. Relationships are supposed to be built on trust," I say, trying to control the anger.

"I know. I was going to tell you on our last date, but I just couldn't bring myself to. I didn't want you to feel alone again," he says, his eyes sparkling with fresh tears. "Madeline, I've had a crush on you for more than a year now. I never thought you would like me the same way, but when I came over here after your accident, I felt how you felt about me. It made me so happy, but I was also worried that if I told you I could read your feelings, it would have freaked you out and made you want to stay away from me."

I let his words sink in for a moment. He's had a crush on me for that long? I've been wasting all this time, being in no rush for a man, but if I'm being honest with myself, why did I reject the thought for so long? Maybe I just thought nobody would be interested in me. Apparently, I was wrong.

"You should have said something earlier because I've had feelings for you for a while now, too." I clear my throat and remind myself about his deception. "Anyway, how did you hide your veins glowing from me for so long?"

"I'm not exactly sure. You didn't really look at me much when I was over here visiting you the first time. You kind of looked at the floor most of the time," he answered, hesitantly. "Our first date was at a dimly lit restaurant, so I don't think you could see it. I was taking the chance on our last date by going out in bright sunlight because like I said, I was planning on telling you. I just didn't get around to saying anything before you were attacked."

"About that. How did you know that guy was going to attack me?"

"I could feel intense hatred radiating off from him. I honestly didn't know he had a knife, but when I saw him walking right towards you with a devious look in his eyes, I stepped in front of you to protect you."

"Why would a complete stranger hate me?" I ask, confused.

"I don't really know. I don't think it was you specifically. My guess is that he was just a coward, and with your broken leg and crutches, you were an easy target. He wasn't right in the head," Ian explains.

"I never did thank you for that. Thank you for saving my life, Ian."

"I would do it again in a heartbeat."

"Let's just hope you won't have to ever again."

"Agreed."

"Okay, so you felt you were helping me by lying. Although, that was a sweet gesture, I want to make it clear right now; I do not tolerate lying. Even if it is to save my feelings. I can tell that you are sorry about doing it, and so I'm willing to forgive you. This time. You have to promise me, Ian, that you will never lie to me like that again. I need to be able to trust you."

"I promise, Madeline," he says, giving me a sincere look. "So, does this mean you might be willing to consider being my girlfriend?"

"I don't know. Are you asking me?" I reply. My heart starts racing a bit.

"Madeline, will you be my girlfriend?"

"Absolutely."

I'm feeling a little silly, like we're in junior high or something. There is an innocence to our conversation that seems to be exactly what I need at this moment. The world has become far too complicated and troubled. It is nice to have a moment of simplicity.

I join him on the couch and we seal it with a kiss. I let out a deep sigh and see that Ian's veins are fading back to a lighter blue.

"Were you just reading my emotions?"

"I can't help it sometimes. Like I said, if they are intense enough, I can't help but feel them."

"Oh? So, what was I feeling then?" I ask, playfully.

"You were feeling happiness, relief, and a little bit of something I think I better not say," he says with a smirk.

I blush and cast my gaze to the floor in embarrassment.

Minutes turn into hours as we are having such a lovely time holding each other and talking about the current events. I let out a groan when the phone rings. I take it in another room.

"Hey, Mads! I hope this is an okay time to talk."

"Not really, Matthew, but go ahead."

"Sorry. Anyway, I have another breakthrough for you. Professor McGreggor told me that they received a report from a team of scientists out of Australia. They found that people who tap into their abilities harder and more frequently, get sick faster and die. I don't have all the information right now for why that is, but I can keep you informed once I do," Matthew offers. "So, I think that's why Elizabeth's husband died. From what you told me, it sounded like he was tapping into his power hardcore every chance he could get, and that's why he had such a rapid descent."

"Really? What about Mrs. Donaldson?" I ask, slightly skeptical.

"Her ability was that she was getting younger, right? She seemed younger to you every time you saw her," Matthew answers.

"That wasn't really her fault though," I say defensively.

"Regardless. She was still tapping into the ability even though she might not have been doing it on a conscious level."

"That's crap! That doesn't seem fair!" I say, raising my voice. I don't mean to yell at Matthew. None of this is his fault, but I'm so angry about this whole stupid powers thing. Mrs. Donaldson shouldn't have had to die.

"I'm sorry, Mads," Matthew says, sounding sad for me.

"How about you? Have you been using yours a lot?"

"No, I wouldn't say a lot, and now that I have the information that I do, I won't be doing it anymore," he promises.

"Oh no, Matthew! Dad was just over here and fixed my leg. His veins were glowing a lot brighter when he left. I just killed Dad!" I say, feeling a little hysterical.

"Calm down. You can't blame yourself. I'm sure Dad will be fine. I'll call him and tell him what I know," he reassures me. I take a deep breath and settle down a bit.

"Hey, listen. Don't tell too many people, okay?" Matthew continues.

"Why not?"

"Professor McGreggor said that the government is trying to keep it a secret because the implication is that this condition is eventually terminal for everyone."

"What!? Is that true?"

"We don't know. Probably not. But if people think it is, there would be complete chaos. I mean, things are barely holding together as it is."

"But people will die! They deserve to know."

"Sorry, Mads. The professor is allowing me to tell my family only because I convinced him that you guys wouldn't tell anyone."

"Okay, but I am going to tell Ian."

"Do what you feel you must do. Just keep it to a bare minimum."

"All right. Thank you. I should probably go. Ian is over here right now."

"Okay, sis. One more thing, do you think you could come down to the lab sometime soon, to give us a blood sample? We would really like to study your blood to see what's different about it."

"Yeah, sure. I'll text you to let you know when I can."

"Okay, great! Talk to you later."

I head back into the living room and sit next to Ian. His veins shine a bit.

"What's the matter, Madeline? You're scared about something," Ian says, looking worried.

"You are going to have to stop that, Ian. That was my brother. He just told me that people who use their abilities more frequently get sick and die faster. Unfortunately, you can't spread the news around, though. He told me that the information isn't being released yet. The government doesn't want there to be even more chaos and panic than there already is."

"I guess that makes sense. I'll keep it to myself."

"And you have to stop using your powers," I plead.

"I'll try, but sometimes I can't control it. If the emotion is strong enough, I read it."

"Just try hard, for me. Please. I don't want to lose you," I say, as I bury my face in his shirt. I inhale deeply, soaking him in as much as I can. It feels so good to finally be able to be intimate with Ian. I just wish I would've known sooner that he liked me. Now I don't know how much time we will have.

"You're going to be the hardest to be around. I want to know what you're feeling. It makes me so happy to know how much you like me."

"Well, let's practice. Try not to read my feelings this time. Kiss me."

He kisses me so passionately that I feel warmth spread throughout my body. Oh gosh, I hope he doesn't read what I'm feeling. Now I'm worried and embarrassed.

When we break apart, I see a brighter shine to his veins.

"This isn't good, Ian. This proximity to me is causing your powers to be tapped. What are we going to do?" I asked, worriedly.

"Well, there really isn't much we can do. I'll try as hard as I can to not read your feelings when I'm around you, but I'm going to keep seeing you. I'm not letting you go, now that I have you," he says with a sweet smile.

A single tear runs down my cheek. He brushes it away with his thumb and gives me a gentle kiss.

"It's going to be all right, Madeline," he says, pulling me close.

I don't know how he can be so sure, but I just let myself melt into his embrace. Maybe things are moving a bit fast, but this all feels so natural, like we have been a couple for a long time.

After seeing Ian's veins glow a couple of more times, I realize that this just isn't going to work. I'm going to have to stop seeing him. I would never be able to live with myself if he ends up dying from this sickness all because of me. Just when I find someone so amazing, I have to give him up, for his own well-being. I know that he isn't going to take this well, so I'm going to just keep it to myself for now.

"Ian, I hate to cut this short, but I'm starting to get a headache," I say. I know I said that I'm against lying, but I'm not really lying. I am actually starting to get one.

"Can I get you anything?"

"No. I think I need to take a nap. I haven't been sleeping the best lately." Which is also true, since I have been having nightmares almost every night.

"Okay," he responds reluctantly, kissing me on the forehead.

I walk him to the door and draw out our goodbye a little, with some extra kissing. I'm really not happy with this plan, but I don't know what else to do. His life is more important than our happiness. I will just have to focus on the hope that someday a cure will be made and we'll get to be together again.

After he leaves, I flop on the couch and shed a few tears out of frustration. I'm really going to have to work hard to not change my mind about this. I try to think of other things to take my thoughts off this depressing situation. I decide that I'm going to pay a little visit to Matthew at his lab, to give him that blood sample. We'll see if he can get an answer to my lack of superpowers and what makes me so different. It may not accomplish much, but I'm getting sick of just waiting around for the world to end. I want to feel like I am at least doing something.

CHAPTER THIRTY

MADELINE

In the morning, as I'm about to hop into my Jeep and head over to the university, I look across the road and see the little neighbor boy throwing a baseball as hard as he can into the air. The ball goes so high I lose sight of it for at least ten seconds before it starts falling out of the clouds, back towards him. The glow in his veins is so bright, I can clearly see it from across the street. I desperately want to go tell him to stop using his powers. The thought of this little boy succumbing to the illness is just too much. But I promised Matthew I wouldn't, so I force myself to just get in the Jeep and drive.

I head over to the university to see Matthew. I texted him first to make sure he would be there. I pull into the parking lot by the science building. I have always loved universities and how they usually look like castles. This building, however, is quite plain on the outside. A large square made of brown bricks. There is nothing terribly exciting about it.

Matthew showed me around the campus a while ago, so I sort of know where I'm going. I head straight to the lab, which is far more interesting to look at than the outside of the building would lead you to believe. I look through the large windows and see a bunch of students buzzing around the stainless-steel tables that are full of beakers, Bunsen burners, and all sorts of other sciencey things I don't know the names to. Matthew must have seen me because he waves and comes to the door to let me in.

"Hey, Sis." Matthew greets me wearing his lab coat and safety goggles. He looks like such a science geek! He even has pens in his pocket with a little blue stain where one leaked. Maybe I should get him a pocket protector for Christmas. I try to restrain a chuckle. "You said you were coming, but you didn't say why? Are you here to give us a sample of your blood?"

"Yes, sir. I was also wondering if you have any more information you could give me about what you were saying over the phone, you know, when you interrupted me making up with Ian?"

"Please, spare me the details on that subject," Matthew says rolling his eyes in jest. I give him a playful shove.

"Do you want my blood sample or should I just leave?" I ask as I pretend to walk away.

"No, no. Stay. I don't really have any more details yet. We're still working it all out. But with a sample of your blood, maybe we can compare what makes yours unique from everyone else's. Are you ready?"

"Yeah, sure" I say reluctantly.

I don't like needles. Who does? But I do want to know what makes me so different.

We leave the university and walk a couple of blocks to the hospital. It only takes us five minutes of waiting for them to call me back and take the sample of blood for my brother. It was quick and relatively painless.

As we are walking back to the university, I take a good look at Matthew to see how bright his veins are now. They don't look too bad, but he has bags under his eyes and looks like he hasn't slept in days. I'm about to chastise him, but I decide to just let it go. We head back into the lab and Matthew takes the blood sample over to the fridge.

"Everyone looks like they're working really hard on something. Is this how it normally is at a university lab?" I ask, making small talk.

"Sometimes, but right now Professor McGreggor is gone. He's with the group of scientists that the government pulled together." Matthew stops to give a big yawn. "I decided to put together my own group of senior students to do what we can here at the lab. We have the professor on Skype at all times so we can keep him informed on what we're doing. He gives us ideas for things to try. I'm not sure we're really going to be able to help in any way, but we've been working around the clock to see if we can assist in finding a cure for this radiation poison. Professor McGreggor said that there's hope for a cure."

"Great! Do you have any idea how a cure can be made for something like this?"

"Of course not. If I did, I would have developed it already."

"Jeez. No need to be a jerk. I was just asking."

"I'm sorry, Mads," Matthew stops to rub is eyes. "I'm just so tired."

"You look tired. How many hours have you been putting into this?"

"Well, I've been going home to sleep, but otherwise I stay here and just keep trying to do what I can to help."

"That doesn't sound healthy, Matthew. Don't work yourself. . ."

"What? To death? If we don't find a cure, Mads, it's only a matter of time before we all die," he snaps. "Sorry."

"Don't worry about it. I would probably be grumpy if I worked as hard as you do," I offer, trying to be understanding. He was willing to forgive me for my outburst at the hospital, I owe him the same consideration.

"Promise me you won't tell Mom. The last time I talked to her, she was freaking out about . . . well, everything. She doesn't need to worry extra about me on top of it all."

"I won't tell Mom. Just make sure you take care of yourself, Matthew. If you die, I'll kill you!" I threaten, playfully, trying hard to make light of the situation.

"I'll try."

"Good. Well, unless you need me for something else, I'll let you get back to work." I'm starting to feel like I'm in the way and distracting Matthew from what he really wants to be doing.

"Thanks for stopping by, Mads. I'll let you know if I find anything out about your blood sample."

"Sounds good."

I make my way back out to the Jeep. Now I'm worried about Matthew working himself too hard. He's a big boy, though. I'm sure he knows his limits.

As I'm driving through Amherst on my way home, I see something strange going on outside of the hardware store. Mr. Bakowski, the hardware store owner, is standing in front of his shop, being shouted at by, Ray, a local guy. I've seen Ray walking around town a lot. He's a clean cut, friendly guy who always says hello and wears a pleasant smile. However, right now, Ray has a murderous glare on his scruffy, unshaven face. By the looks of him, he hasn't showered or washed his clothes in weeks. Before I pass by, he punches Mr. Bakowski in the face, knocking him to the ground. I stop my Jeep and watch as Ray leans over and takes Mr. Bakowski's wallet out of his back pocket. I can't let him get away with this!

"Hey! Give him his wallet back, or I'm calling the cops!" I shout, holding up my cell phone.

Ray spins around and looks in my direction. He gives me a nasty look, crouches down, and leaps over the store and out of sight.

I hop out of my Jeep and run over to Mr. Bakowski.

"Hey, are you okay?"

He sits up rubbing the side of his face where he got punched.

"Yeah, I . . . I think so."

I offer him my hand to help him stand up.

"Do you want me to call the police for you?" I offer.

"No. That's all right."

"But he just assaulted you! Are you sure?"

"Look, I know Ray. He's a good guy. He would never have done this if it weren't for the sickness going around. I have faith that he will return my wallet."

"Why would he do that?"

"Because I don't have anything in it," he says with a sly grin, but then grimaces and rubs his sore cheek.

"What about your driver's license or credit cards?"

"Nope. I leave all that locked away in a safe upstairs in my apartment. I rarely drive anywhere. Everything I need is in walking distance. I just carry this empty wallet out of habit. I kind of wish I could see his face when he opens it," he chuckles to himself.

I smile along with him.

"Thanks for speaking up and trying to stop it from happening. That was brave of you. I just wish I had a power that could have stopped him."

"What are your powers, if you don't mind me asking?" I now notice that he hardly has any blue glow under his olive skin.

"I guess you could say that I'm a human chameleon. My skin changes color to match my surroundings."

He puts his hand on the wall of the hardware store and his hand turns red to match the paint.

"You shouldn't . . . I mean, cool" I say, almost letting slip what Matthew told me. I really hope they find a way to make the dangers of using powers public.

"Eh, it's not terribly useful. When kids come in my store, they seem to think it's neat, but other than that, I couldn't care less."

"I should probably get going. Are you going to be all right?"

"Yeah, it was just one blow. I've had worse in my day," he chuckles. "Thanks again for the help."

Once I'm back home, I lock the door behind me and turn on the TV. I'd like to see if there are news reports warning people against using their powers yet. I almost let it slip to Mr. Bakowski. I'm not sure how much longer I can keep it to myself. I see my answer right away. Looks like the information has been released. All the stations have a ticker scrolling a warning against using superpowers. Suddenly, the news report catches my attention.

"*. . . pandemonium across the globe. Reports show that vast numbers of people are dying from this radiation poisoning. We strongly urge that everyone stops using their powers immediately. I repeat stop using your powers. Using your superpower causes the radiation poison to spread more rapidly throughout your body, ultimately resulting in death.*"

I turn the TV off and lay back in my chair. What happens if nobody finds a cure to this? Will I end up being the only one left alive? I probably stand out now when I go out in public. I don't have glowing blue veins. I feel so guilty that I don't have to deal with this like everyone else.

My heart feels heavy in my chest. Why did this have to happen? Is this the end of the world?

Ring!

I jump.

Ring!

I pick up my cell phone and answer it.

"Hello?"

"Goose, your father's in the hospital. He took a turn for the worse," my mom says, through tears.

"No! Please tell me you're joking."

"I'm not. You need to come soon before it's too . . . "

"Stop. I'll be right there" I interrupt. I don't want to hear the rest of what she was about to say.

I hang up the phone and run out to my Jeep, tears welling up in my eyes. Guilt is weighing heavy on my mind. My father is going to die and it is all my fault.

CHAPTER THIRTY-ONE

MADELINE

I race to the hospital. I am so afraid of what I'm about to see, I feel sick to my stomach. I stop at the nurses' station and ask where I can find my dad.

"Down the hall, third door to your right," she says quickly.

"Thank you."

I hurry down the hall and find my mother standing in the doorway. I give her a hug and hold her tight. Her veins are brighter than the last time I saw her, but they still don't seem too bad.

We walk into the hospital room and I see my dad lying on the bed. His veins are glowing just as brightly as when he left my house after fixing my leg, but he's at least conscious.

"Oh Dad! I am so sorry. This is all my fault."

"Nonsense, Madeline. How is this your fault?"

"If you hadn't fixed my leg, you wouldn't be here right now. I wish I could make things all better for you," I say, leaning down and giving him a big hug.

"Well, what's done is done. I'm happy to see you walking around again, Marie."

"Madeline."

"What?"

"You just called me Marie. That's Mom's name."

"I did? Oh, sorry."

Just then, a nurse comes in to check on my dad, and my mom pulls me off to the side to talk.

"This isn't the first time he has gotten confused. He called me by his sister's name the other day. He also put his dirty dishes in the fridge and put soap on his toothbrush," my mom sighs. "I don't like this."

I choose not to tell my mom this, but I think what she is describing is another sign of deterioration from the radiation poisoning. People go crazy or confused before becoming fatally ill. Mrs. Donaldson never realized she was being rude to me.

"Dad hasn't become verbally abusive or mean lately, has he?"

"No, thank goodness. I would hate to see that happen. Your father has always been so kind and loving. It would break my heart if he started being mean before the end," she manages to say before crying.

"Dad isn't going to die. Matthew says that they're trying hard to find a cure. Maybe they'll figure something out soon, before it's too late."

"I hope so," she sniffles.

"Marie?" my dad says.

"Yes, dear?" she responds, walking back over his bed.

"Where are the children?"

"What children?"

"Why, Matthew and Madeline, of course."

My mom points at me, "That's Madeline, Charles." Fresh tears are rolling down her face again. My father looks at me completely confused.

"Madeline? How can this be? You're a woman. What happened to my little girl?"

"It's me, Dad," I say, taking his hand into mine.

He stares at me, searching my face for recognition and finally something seems to click.

"Oh, Madeline. How's your leg?"

"It's fine, thank you," I say giving him a weak smile. "Dad, do you know where you are?"

He looks around the room and responds, "It looks like a hospital. Why am I in a hospital?"

How do I break this to him? I guess I just give him the facts and see what happens.

"The world was blasted with radiation from a star that went supernova. Everyone, except me, got superpowers, but the more people use them, the faster they get sick," I explain.

"I have superpowers? What can I do?" he asks. His eyes lighting up with excitement.

"You have the power to heal people, but after you healed my leg, your veins were glowing extremely bright, and now you're sick."

"I don't feel sick. I feel just fine," he says as he tries to get out of bed.

"Charles, you need to stay in bed," my mom says, pushing him back down gently.

"Are you a nurse?" he asks my mom, a child-like dreamy look on his face.

"No, I'm your wife."

"Hmm. I don't remember getting married but okay. You're pretty," he says with a smile.

My mom is beside herself with grief. I tell her to go take a little walk to calm down.

After she leaves, I sit back down by my father.

"Madeline, I feel like I'm going crazy," my dad says with fear in his eyes. "It's like I keep slipping in and out of consciousness, but I know I'm not falling asleep. I can't remember things anymore."

"It's going to be okay, Dad. Matthew said that they are trying to find a cure for this. We'll get you fixed in no time."

"I sure hope so. I hate to see your mother cry so much. I don't want to be a burden to her."

"You're not a burden. She just loves you and doesn't want to see anything bad happen to you."

I'm thankful to be having a somewhat lucid conversation with my dad. I tell him about making up with Ian. He seems happy for me, but a little less willing to forgive Ian so quickly, since he caused me emotional distress. There he goes being that over protective father again. Oh well. To be honest, I don't mind. It makes me feel loved. After a while, he gets sleepy and asks if it's all right for him to take a nap. I reassure him that I'll stay by his side until Mom gets back.

I sit in the ugly, stained hospital chair, looking at my father's face, hoping this won't be the last memory I have of him; laying in a hospital bed, slowly losing his mind. For something to do, I start to compare my features to my father's. I definitely have his nose, which is bigger than my mother's small, slightly upturned nose. His lips are thinner than mine and his eyes are closer together, but his round face perfectly matches my own. A tear runs down my cheek. How soon is the sickness going to take him?

Once Mom comes back, I tell her about my conversation with Dad. It seems to make her feel a little better. We talk for a while before I decide to head home. I can't handle much more of seeing my father fall apart. The guilt is tearing me apart inside. I feel guilty that I'm the one that caused this to happen to him, that I'm leaving my mother alone to deal with this by herself, and that I appear to be the only one who doesn't have to face this deteriorating sickness. There is nothing I can do about any of it.

I head home and find a message on my answering machine. It's from Elizabeth.

"I'm sorry this is such short notice, Madeline. Things are so crazy right now. We're having Philip's funeral tomorrow afternoon at one o'clock. It's at the church Philip and I got married in. It seemed fitting. I hope you aren't busy because I would really like you to be there. See you tomorrow."

When I had talked to Ian on the phone earlier, he had said something about coming over tomorrow. At the time, I didn't have any excuse to give him for not coming, but this will be a good one. There will be too many people with strong emotions at the funeral for him to try to tag along. It is becoming harder and harder to find reasons for him to not come see me. I know I'm doing this for his own good, but damn it, I miss him.

CHAPTER THIRTY-TWO

VINCENT

Vincent wakes up to the glare of the mid-morning sun shining through the car window on his face. He sits up and rolls his neck, trying to get the kinks out. He had driven a little way out of town to a small park. He decided it was as good of a place as any to park his car for the night to sleep.

He pushes open the door and steps out, taking a deep breath of fresh air. As he stretches out his sore muscles, he looks around. It's not much of a park really. It's more of a parking lot for a bike trail entrance. He spots a picnic table over by the river and has a small breakfast of warm beer and stale donuts.

I gotta figure out what I'm gonna do. I should leave town, but we drove all this way . . . and I still want revenge for my little girl! No. I need to find this Madeline chick and finish the job quick before they find Frank's body. I think I'll take a little drive around town and see if I can spot her.

Vincent makes his way slowly around town, driving down every road, but doesn't see her. He finds the public library Dani had told him that Madeline works at. It's closed and doesn't open until two in the afternoon.

Damn it! Where the hell is she? Probably having a meeting with her government friends, trying to figure out some other way to screw my life over.

He makes his way to the grocery store to buy some fresh food. On his way out, he sees a newspaper stand and snatches one up when he sees the headline, "Scientists Solve the Blackout Mystery".

He paces back and forth as he reads the article.

Lies! They're trying to blame it on a Supernova? The scientists sayin' this are more than likely in the back pocket of the government. It's all a cover up for what's really goin' on. Distraction and control!

Once he's done reading the article, he crumples the newspaper out of disgust, drops it, and turns around to leave.

"Hey! You have to pay for that!" The store clerk yells at him.

Vincent turns around, sneers at him, and shoots a lightning bolt at the paper, lighting it on fire. The clerk scrambles to grab the fire extinguisher from behind the service desk, giving Vincent the opportunity to leave. He drives back to the small park again.

He parks the car, pops open a cold beer, and leans his head against the headrest, closing his eyes for a moment.

"What now, Vinny?" Vincent hears.

He looks at the passenger seat and there's Frank, his dead eyes looking straight at him. Vincent squeezes his own eyes shut, and starts pounding his head with his fists.

"You ain't real. Go away!" Vincent screams.

"Of course I ain't real, you moron. You let me die in that crappy motel room. But I can still talk some sense into ya. Why don't you just pack it up and head home?"

"Now why would I go and do that? We came all this way, I might as well finish the job."

"I told ya I had a vision of some girl from Wisconsin and you dimwits drive across the country on a hunch, in hopes of killin' her. Your floozy said she works at the library. She ain't no government agent."

"Yeah, well, that's gotta just be a cover. You said you seen a vision of her in a lab talkin' to other scientists. What would a librarian be doing in a lab, Frankie," Vincent asks. "Frank?"

He turns to look at the passenger seat, and Frank is gone.

"Aw hell! Now where'd ya go?" Vincent gets out of the car and scans the area looking for Frank. "Frank? Where are ya, man?" Vincent calls out. He sees a trail leading through the woods.

He musta went that way.

Vincent starts walking at a brisk pace to try to catch up with Frank.

"Frank, where'd ya go?" Vincent yells, frantically searching for his buddy. He stops dead in his tracks.

What the hell am I doin'? Frank is dead! I'm losin' my frickin' mind!

He turns around and runs back to the car, locking the doors for good measure.

Oh God! What just happened? I thought Frank was actually here speakin' to me? I keep forgettin' my name, or where I am, and now I think my dead friend is really havin' conversations with me?

Vincent closes his eyes, and takes a few deep breaths to try to settle himself down. He can feel the tension slowly releasing from his muscles. The next thing he knows, it's afternoon.

CHAPTER THIRTY-THREE

MADELINE

It's the day of the funeral and I put on my black dress clothes. I head over to the church. There doesn't seem to be many cars. Maybe I heard her wrong and I'm early.

Once inside the church, I see Elizabeth standing up front by Philip's casket. She is wiping her eyes with a tissue. She spots me and walks over to greet me.

"Madeline. I'm so glad you were able to come," she says through tears. I give her a big hug.

"Am I early? You said one o'clock, right?" I ask, looking around.

There are only about ten people here.

"You're not early. I don't think there are going to be many people here. There are not a lot of people fit to come to this. So many of our friends and family are sick," Elizabeth says, looking distraught.

I give her another big hug, and then she leads me to the front to pay my respects. I have never liked seeing people in caskets. It creeps me out because I always imagine their eyes popping open. I wonder if his entire eyes are blue like the dead people in my dream. I shiver at the thought. Elizabeth glances at me, so I rub my bare arms with my hands, pretending that I am cold to mask my uneasiness.

A few more people show up, but not many. Some of the ones that do, seem to be losing it. There's one person that appears to have lost complete control of his power. He apparently has the ability to start fires. He keeps lighting the pew in front of him on fire, but he puts it out right away with a fire extinguisher that he brought along with him. There are random mumblings going on behind me, and I just ignore it until they start laughing out loud. I turn around and see someone pointing at the ceiling rafters, but when I look up, there is nothing there. Funerals are bad enough, but this is starting to feel like a horror movie.

Finally, it's over.

"We're not having a meal or anything," Elizabeth says, looking around at the guests filing out of the church. "We didn't think it would be such a great idea . . . considering . . ."

"Gotcha. Do you want me to come over and keep you company?" I ask.

"Nah. I think I want to just head home and take a nap or something."

"Okay," I say, giving her a big hug. "Call me if you need anything."

Once I get home, I remember that I had turned off my cell phone for the funeral. After it's on, I see that Matthew left a message for me. He sounds excited.

"Hey, Mads. We were studying your blood sample and we found something interesting. I can't really explain it over the phone, but I was wondering if you could come back to the lab. They think it might be possible to use your blood to make a cure!"

CHAPTER THIRTY-FOUR

VINCENT

I *musta fallen asleep. Time to go make another trip through town.*
He drives up and down every street, looking for Madeline. He stops by the library and sees that the lights are on. He parks the car and heads inside.

Crap! That's not her, he thinks when he sees Mrs. Yates behind the counter.

"Can I help you?" Mrs. Yates asks.

"Is Madeline here?"

"No, she doesn't work today."

"Do ya know where I can find her?"

"Sie ist wahrscheinlich zu Hause jetzt," Mrs. Yates says, smiling.

"What did you just say?" Vincent says, annoyed.

This batty old woman's messin' with me.

"Je suis désolé. Voulez-vous que je parle plus fort?" Mrs. Yates says slowly, raising her voice. She looks at Vincent as though waiting for him to respond.

"Whatever! I'll find her myself!" Vincent says, storming out.

He gets back in the car and keeps driving. He makes his way over to a street lined with duplexes. He's halfway down the road when he spots a young woman with coppery red hair come bolting out of her house, jump into a Jeep, and speed away.

Was that her? She's the only red headed woman I've seen in town, but Frank said she had a broken leg. This chick doesn't. I'll follow her anyway and see where she goes.

CHAPTER THIRTY-FIVE

MADELINE

I get to the lab as fast as I can. My heart is pounding out of my chest. I pray that Matthew is right about this. I don't know what he found in my blood, but I hope his idea works.

I run through the lab doors and find Matthew talking animatedly with another guy in a lab coat. They end their conversation and he rushes over to me.

"So, what's going on? What did you find?" I ask.

"Well, when everyone was hit with the radiation, it damaged the plasma cells within the bone marrow, which is where the plasma cells originate. The plasma cells started producing large quantities of a special paraprotein."

"You pretty much explained that to me already," I say, hoping he'll get to the point.

"Yes, well, this special paraprotein, we called it SN-protein, short for supernova protein, binds to DNA forming a coating, of sorts, over the top of the DNA strands. This caused an epigenetic effect," he pauses, clearly waiting for me to react surprised or shocked.

"You do realize that I have no idea what that means, right?" I respond, trying not to get frustrated.

"Sorry. How do I explain this to you . . ." he says stroking his chin thoughtfully. "All right, epigenetics is when a gene changes expression, or in other words, how the DNA behaves, without actually changing the DNA. The SN-protein bonds to the DNA without necessarily damaging it, it just changes how our genes behave. Which, apparently, amplifies any latent potential that is already there . . . That's what gave us all our superpowers."

"Okay. So, what about me? I was blasted with the same radiation. Didn't that happen to me too?"

"Well, your DNA strands are completely normal. There appears to be no SN-protein coating on them anywhere. The supernova radiation did cause you to have MGUS though, just like the rest of us, only your body created a different kind of paraprotein."

"Great," I say sarcastically, allowing my frustration to show. It is hard to understand what all of this means.

"Let me sum this up. Supernova radiation damage to plasma cells . . . " Matthew explains, ticking his fingers, "production of a paraprotein we named SN-protein . . . SN-protein bonded with our DNA strands and the bond caused a coating over the DNA strands that didn't damage the DNA, it just changed how the DNA behaved. This is where the superpowers come from. Your plasma cells also produce a paraprotein; but one that is different from the rest of us."

"All right. What makes me different?"

"I have a theory. I need to look into it further, but I believe you have a unique mutation in your DNA that changed the make-up of your plasma cells and the way they behave."

"A mutation? I'm a mutant?" I say, making a sad attempt at humor.

"No. You are not a mutant. As I said, this is just a theory right now, but it looks as though you had a mutation before the supernova even happened. This mutation would have just been another harmless cell mutation that laid dormant in your system, but then the supernova happened. You got MGUS just like the rest of us, affecting your plasma cells to start producing a paraprotein, but because of your cell mutation, your plasma cells didn't create SN-protein, it created something entirely different."

"What do you mean?" I hate having to ask a million questions.

"When I was looking at your blood, I could see that there was a similar excess of paraproteins in your sample, but unlike the SN-proteins everyone else has, yours have not bonded to your DNA in any way. They appeared to be benign or useless. It was not immediately clear as to why your paraproteins were behaving so differently. We started isolating some of them to do a direct comparison with the SN-proteins we have already cataloged, but this can take some time. So while we were waiting, I started running some other lab tests. I extracted some of the paraproteins from the plasma in your blood sample and added it to a small sample of my blood and something amazing happened! I watched as your special paraproteins bonded themselves with my SN-protein. Can you believe it?" he says, as though his words mean something to me. My expression must have indicated that, once again, I was not following him.

He lets out a sigh. It is obviously hard for him to have to try to explain these things in terms that I could understand. I suddenly feel grateful that Matthew has always been so patient with me when trying to explain things I don't get.

"You see Mads, paraproteins or antibodies, are part of your immune system."

"Okay." Immune system, at least I am familiar with that term.

"But they don't actually remove infections from the system. What they do is bond to invasive components, called antigens, in the body so that the rest of your immune system can target the foreign bodies to be removed. If an antibody can't bond to a virus, for instance, then your immune system can't identify the virus as something that needs to be removed. The fact that your paraprotein bonded with my SN-protein implies that it may be possible to construct a treatment that would allow each individual's own immune system to remove the SN-proteins as if they were some kind of virus. If this works without damaging the DNA, we could cure the radiation poisoning!"

"That is amazing!" I say, finally seeing why he is so excited.

"It is!" Matthew agrees. "We'd like to do more tests with your plasma, to try to figure out how to utilize it and develop a cure. We are going to need you to start donating plasma."

"Sure. Anything I can do to help."

"Great! We'd like to get you started right away. We've called a company named Biochem, which is a plasma donating center. There happens to be one nearby. I'll go with you and take the plasma they extract back here to the lab to get started on this right away."

CHAPTER THIRTY-SIX

VINCENT

Vincent carefully follows Madeline into the science building and stands outside of the laboratory windows, watching in awe as Frank's vision unfolds, just as he said it would. A young red headed girl talking to a guy in the lab who seems to be really excited about something.

I just wish I could hear what he's sayin'.

Just then, the lab door opens as a student comes out.

"Hey, you! Who's that?" Vincent asks the sleepy-eyed student, pointing towards Madeline.

"Oh, I think her name is Madeline," he yawns. "She's the sister of Matthew . . ."

"Is Matthew the one in charge around here?" Vincent interrupts.

"No, Matthew's a senior here at the University. You're looking for Professor McGreggor," the student answers, pushing his safety glasses back up on his nose.

"Where's he at?" Vincent says.

"He's not here. He's in Chicago having an important meeting with other head scientists from around the world. The government called them together," the geeky student says, gushing. He's clearly impressed with the professor. "It's a real honor. Professor McGreggor is one of the smartest scientists I know . . ."

Vincent turns around and stomps out of the building, back to his car. He climbs inside and punches the steering wheel.

"What the hell, Frank? All this time, we thought it was the girl who was important. Instead, it's the girl's brother's professor who's in league with the government. This chick has nothin' to do with any of it! If you weren't dead, I'd slap you right now!"

Vincent starts driving, fuming about his wasted efforts. He glances at the picture of Maggie he taped to the dash board. His heart aches when he sees her little face smiling so brightly. He sighs.

I guess it was a connection, however small of one. No point in sticking around now. I'm gonna go find this professor and all his government friends and show them what I think of all these lies and manipulation. But first, I'm gonna make a little stop by Pete's ol' friend. See if I can't get a little somethin' to surprise the professor and those government rats with.

CHAPTER THIRTY-SEVEN

MADELINE

We walk into the building and it smells clean, like a medical clinic. A lady in a lab coat leads me straight to what she calls a bed, but it is more like a solid reclining chair. She explains that normally they would have to check my blood first for a protein count and iron levels to make sure I am fit for donating. However, they're not going to bother with that under the circumstances.

Overall, it isn't that bad of an experience. I hate needles and this needle is kind of big, but the lady seems to know what she's doing and is able to get it into my arm without hurting too much. The medicine, or "anticoagulation chemical" as the nurse called it, that the machine adds to my blood before pumping it back into my body, makes my lips tingle a bit and my arm starts to cramp from all the arm flexing I have to do while the machine takes my blood, but otherwise, once I'm done, I feel pretty good.

Matthew has been waiting up front in the waiting room. The lady brings him the bottle of my plasma, and he puts it in the cooler that he brought along. We thank the nurse and head outside to the parking lot.

"Thank you for doing this, Mads," Matthew says, giving me a hug.

"Of course, if it means saving the world, not to mention, Dad."

"Now, you should wait a day between donations to make sure you replenish your fluids. Drink extra water, Mads. We are kind of asking a lot from you. Usually, they only allow people to donate two times a week, but we are in dire straits. We need you to donate every other day until we figure out if it's really going to work and if we can find a way to mass produce it in a lab. We will need quite a bit for all the additional experiments we will need to run. If you start getting dehydrated, we can have you come in for an IV between the days you donate."

"We'll see how I feel, and I can decide later."

"I need you to be okay, Mads. This is an incredible thing you're doing. Normally, I wouldn't tell you this to your face, but I love you, Sis" he says, playfully.

"Yeah, yeah, love you too," I say with a smirk. "I don't feel like I'm really doing anything incredible. I'm only donating plasma, which other people do all the time."

"True, other people donate and they get compensated for it. You are going to be donating a whole lot more than they do and you won't be getting paid money. You will be doing this out of the kindness of your heart," Matthew points out.

"Regardless, it is you that is doing something incredible. If you develop a cure, Matthew, you'll be saving what's left of the entire world!"

"Maybe. We have to see if this works first. Speaking of which, I should probably get back to the lab and get to work. I really hope my theory is right," he is almost shaking with excitement.

"Me too. Call me as soon as you figure it out."

"Sure thing. Bye!"

He hops in his car and takes off. A wave of relief washes over me and for the first time in a long time; it feels like maybe everything will be all right.

CHAPTER THIRTY-EIGHT

MADELINE

Waiting.

That is what my life has become now. An agonizing waiting game as I keep hoping for Matthew to tell me that they really did find a cure. I go to Biochem to donate plasma every other day as planned. So far, so good. On the days I donate, I stop by the hospital to check up on my dad. His health and memory are continuing to get worse every time I see him. Yesterday, he believed that he was still in college. He refused to believe my mom when she told him he was married to her and had Matthew and me. He started muttering something about missing his Calculus with Analytic Geometry class and that the professor was going to give him an F for being late again. He then laid his head back on his pillow and instantly started snoring.

I hope Matthew figures this out soon. It's been killing me trying to come up with excuses to avoid Ian, when all I want, is to be with him.

Elizabeth finally scheduled a doctor's appointment. She asked me to go with her. They did an ultrasound to make sure everything is all right with her baby. The baby is healthy, thank God. It's still too early to tell what the gender of the baby is, but I just have this gut feeling that it's going to be a boy.

We spent the rest of the day just hanging out. Elizabeth tries to hide it, but she is still struggling with the grief of losing Philip. There is a sadness in her eyes that breaks my heart. I'm not sure what I would do if Ian died, and I have only been dating him for a little over a month. The fact that she can function somewhat normally, blows my mind.

Today is a donating day. I'm getting used to the process now. The needle doesn't even bother me that much anymore. Once I'm done, I head over to the hospital.

My mom seems to be kind of a basket case today. This is all so incredibly hard on her. We sit down next to my father, who is sleeping right now, and I suggest that we say a nice long prayer. We take our time and try to include everyone we can think of. I can tell that she feels a bit better afterward, at least calmer anyway.

"I hate to admit this, but I had thoughts about using my powers until I got to be in the same state as your father. The thought of living without him is just too much to bear." Mom says, casting her eyes down in shame.

"I guess I can understand that, but please don't. I love you, Mom," I say squeezing her shoulder. A peaceful quiet falls over us as we sit together watching my dad sleep.

After a while, I stand up to stretch a bit. "I think I'm going to go down to the coffee shop and grab something to eat. Would you like me to get you anything?"

"No thanks, Goose."

As I make my way down to the hospital entrance, I can't help but notice people are staring at me. Some of them look like they're angry.

A little kid with bright veins points at me and says, "Look, Mommy! She doesn't have blue glowing veins." Everyone in his vicinity stops and glares at me.

I speed up. I'm almost to the front when someone grabs my arm and spins me around.

"Why don't you have the same thing as the rest of us? Huh? You got some secret? You better tell me what it is or I'll make you suffer!" says a crazed man with an evil smile. I feel his fingers crushing my arm like a vice. I struggle, but can't break free from his grip. He tightens his grip even more and I cry out in pain.

"Let go of me! I don't have any secrets!" I yell, clenching my free hand into a fist. Perhaps if I hit him hard enough in the face, I can get away. Before I do, someone grabs the crazy man's other arm, twists it around his back, and puts him in a choke hold. That someone is Ian.

"Let her go!" Ian shouts. The man looks stunned and releases his grip on me. I step back from him, rubbing my arm.

"What? Who are you? What's going on?" says the man, now looking scared.

"You just attacked me!" I yell at him. I don't care if he is confused because of the sickness. I am so upset right now. This is the second time someone has tried to hurt me. I'm really getting tired of this. Thank God, Ian is here to save me once again.

"I don't remember attacking you. I'm sorry, Miss," the man says, tears welling up in his eyes.

Ian lets the man go towards the door, but he positions himself between me and my bewildered attacker. Everyone that was standing around watching goes back about their business as though nothing happened.

"Come on, Madeline. Let's get out of here." Ian grabs my hand, and we start walking quickly. What's Ian doing here? I take a good look at him and his veins are shining brightly. I start to panic.

"Ian! Your veins! See, I knew it was bad for you to be around me!"

"You've been avoiding me, haven't you? That's why you always have an excuse to not see me," Ian says looking hurt.

"It's true. I'm sorry, Ian. I got scared the last time you were with me and I kept seeing your veins glowing. I knew you wouldn't agree to stop seeing each other, for your own sake. I felt that I needed to protect you, to keep you at a distance, so that you wouldn't get sicker," I say.

"Well, that sucks. I've been losing control of when my powers get used, no matter who I'm with. Just the other day, I was picking up some groceries, and I was suddenly feeling everybody's emotions when I walked passed them. I couldn't make it stop."

"So that explains why your veins are so much brighter than the last time I saw you." I say realizing that the blueness hasn't faded away like it was doing before. He's getting farther along in the stages of sickness. Fear starts taking over my mind. Not Ian too!

"Madeline, I want to be with you. Your avoiding me only lost us precious time together. If I'm going to lose my life to this sickness, then I want to be spending every second I can with you. That's why I'm here. I saw you leave to donate this morning and remembered that you said you stop at the hospital to check on your dad when you're done. I thought maybe it would be good if I meet your parents, too. When you told me on our last phone call, that your father was getting worse, I knew I needed to come here sooner rather than later."

We make it to my father's room. I stop and give Ian a quick kiss before we go in.

"My brother is working on a cure. I'm hopeful that he'll be able to do it. I just hope he finishes it soon. Not only for my dad, but now for your sake, too."

"And the rest of the world," Ian chuckles, leaning in close.

We stand with our foreheads together. I feel like I'm being extremely selfish. He's right. The whole world needs a cure, but here I am, only worrying about my loved ones and their fate. I can't help it. I need them.

"I hope you won't think this is too soon, Madeline but I feel like I should say it before it's too late," he says, pausing a moment. "I love you."

I feel goosebumps run down my body. Before Ian, I always wondered how you would know when you fell in love with someone. Was it a mental thing? A physical thing? Would you just suddenly know? Or would it take years before you realized it?

Right now, I have no doubts. I just know. I know with all my being. I can feel every part of me buzzing with a kind of excitement I've never felt before.

"I love you too, Ian."

He breathes a sigh of relief and we kiss. I'm so caught up in the moment, I temporarily forgot the urgency of getting back to my father's room. It isn't until a nurse passes us and I feel her staring at me, that I grab Ian's hand and pull him into the room. I quickly close the door behind us.

"Mom, this is Ian. Ian this is my mom and that's my dad," I say, pointing to my dad. He is still asleep.

Ian walks over to my mom and shakes her hand.

"I'm so glad I finally get to meet you, Ian. Madeline has told me so much about you."

Ian smiles. "Good things, I hope."

"Of course."

While Ian is looking over at my dad, my mom mouths, "He's cute!" I nod my head in agreement.

"Someone tried to attack me in the lobby," I tell my mom. "I was getting a bunch of dirty looks from people, too."

"Why?" she says, almost leaping back off her chair.

"Everyone seems to notice that I'm the only one without blue glowing veins and with so many people not being in their right mind, it apparently makes them hate me."

"That is just. . ."

"Crazy, right? There seems to be a lot of that going around."

Just then, my phone rings.

"I gotta take this."

As I'm walking to the door, I hear my mom say, "So, Ian. Tell me a little about yourself." I decide that the hallway doesn't seem safe, so I just stop by the hanging curtains next to the door.

"Hey, Matthew. What's up?"

"I just thought I would call you with an update. While doing trials, I decided to try giving myself a shot of your plasma, just to see what happened. I monitored my arm for a couple of hours and the area directly around the injection site started to lose the blue glow."

"So you're cured!?" I feel a wave of excitement.

"No," he answers. His reply crushes my spirit as fast as it had lifted. "But this was an important step. This strongly indicates that a cure can be developed. The reduction of the blue glow was the best-case scenario." It is refreshing to hear the optimism in his voice.

"I have a question about that. The blue glow. Why is there a blue glow?"

"It would appear that the SN-protein has what's called bioluminescence. You commonly see it in marine life, like squids or jelly fish. Somehow the radiation damage caused the SN-protein to be imbued with this characteristic. When people access the SN-protein coated DNA, or superpower DNA, it activates the bioluminescence and causes a chemical reaction that makes their plasma glow brighter."

"I guess that is kind of cool, if it wasn't for the whole getting sick and dying part."

"Yeah, about that. We think we have a better understanding of why that happens. When someone accesses their power, it alerts the damaged plasma cells that the SN-protein is 'needed' because it's being used. The plasma cells then produce more and more of the SN-protein, spreading it further throughout the body. As I said, it coats our DNA, changing the way it behaves, but as the levels increase, so does the potency of the epigenetic affects. Initially this causes people's powers to increase, but it doesn't take long and the maximum tolerance levels of the underlying DNA is exceeded. At that point, the DNA no longer provides normal cell functions."

"So that's why everyone starts to act strangely and eventually dies? Because their cells no longer function the way they are supposed to?"

"Correct. Now, as I was saying before, based on this positive test, I think I have an idea how to use your plasma to develop a cure. I haven't tried it yet, but I'm going to do a process called plasmapheresis."

Here we go again with a bunch of scientific things I don't understand.

"What's that?" I ask.

"Plasmapheresis is a process done to exchange plasma in the blood. We will be removing a portion of my plasma and then replace it with a batch of yours. If my theory is correct, that should allow your vast amount of special paraprotein to travel throughout my entire body and attach themselves to the SN-protein. My immune system will then kick into gear, attack it, and eradicate it."

"Awesome!" I stop to think for a moment. "Wait, won't your body just make more SN-protein?"

"Ah, very clever. You see, you're not as dumb as you look." Matthew teases.

"Ha . . . ha . . . ha," I say, shaking my head even though he can't see me.

"You're right, though. My damaged plasma cells will most likely keep manufacturing the protein. But the hope is that with a large enough dosage of your paraproteins, my immune system will fully kick in and begin to see the SN-protein as an intruder. It will begin to mimic your paraproteins and start making antibodies on its own that will continue the process. Think of it like a vaccine, but one that requires a massive dose."

I pause. The weight of what he is saying suddenly hits me. "Hold on! If this works, how are you going to have enough to cure everyone, Matthew? I'm only one person," I say, overwhelmed by the sheer number of people that would need my plasma.

"Not to worry, Mads. We are already manufacturing your special paraprotein through hybridoma technology. With you continuing to donate, and scientists culturing it in a lab, if this works, they will be making it in labs all over the country. We will be able to have enough over time."

"What happens to you if this doesn't work?"

"Most likely, I would just feel sick for a few days, and then I go back to the drawing board and try to race the clock once again."

"Call me as soon as you find out if it works or not."

"Will do. Hey, how is Dad doing?"

"Okay, I guess. He hasn't woken up at all since I got here."

"Well, let me know if anything changes. I should go so I can get the plasmapheresis started. Talk to you soon, Sis."

I head back into the room and fill everyone in on what Matthew just told me. I try my hardest to explain all the technical stuff. I'm still not sure I understand it completely. They seem to understand the gist of it.

Ian and I stay and talk with my mom for another hour or so. My dad has still not woken up, which starts to worry me. Ian asks me if I want to head out to go grab something to eat. My mom seems a little more calm and hopeful after hearing what Matthew is doing, so I agree to go.

Please, dear God, let Matthew get this to work!

CHAPTER THIRTY-NINE

MADELINE

It has been a full day now and I still haven't heard back from Matthew. I find myself pacing around my duplex, willing my phone to ring. This has to work. I don't know how much longer my father, or Ian, has before the sickness takes their lives. Ian's veins are glowing so brightly now. When I kissed him goodnight outside his front door last night, he was pretty much glowing in the dark. He's been acting a little strange too. I had to remind him who I was a couple of times yesterday. He also thought my duplex was his and when he went to go change clothes, he couldn't figure out why there were so many girly shirts in "his" closet. He has been short with me a few times, too. He apologizes right away after sensing my hurt feelings, but I know that reading my emotions is only going to make his condition worse.

Hurry up, Matthew!

Just when I think that maybe I should text Matthew, my phone rings. But it's not him.

"Goose, your father isn't waking up! The doctor said he's in a coma."

"No! He needs to hold on just a little while longer." The all too familiar feeling of fear washes over me again. It wasn't long after Mrs. Donaldson went into a coma that she woke up and then died. This can't happen to my father. It will be my fault that he died. He told me not to think that way, but I can't help it. If I hadn't been so stupid and hurt myself, my father wouldn't have had to fix me and damage himself in the process.

"Matthew better hurry up. I'm not sure how much longer he has," Mom says, her voice breaking.

"I'll be right there, Mom."

I make it to my father's room without incident this time. I hold my mom's hand as we sit and stare at my father lying motionless in bed. The heart monitor beeps rhythmically and his chest rises and falls with his breathing, but those are the only indications that he's still alive.

More waiting.

I find that I had dozed off, when my phone rings and startles me awake.

It's Matthew. Finally!

"It worked! I'm cured!"

"Oh, thank God! Great work, Matthew! Why did it take so long?"

"I had to give my body's immune system enough time to attack the SN-protein. Once my veins were no longer glowing, I took a blood sample to study and found that there was no more SN-protein coating anywhere on my DNA. Not even a trace. I checked to make sure my superpower was gone and it was."

"Great! Is there any way you can do this for Dad now? He's in a coma, Matthew."

"What?! Why didn't you let me know?"

"Mom just called me this morning, and I didn't want to interrupt you. I wanted you to stay focused and let you have time to find a cure."

"I'll contact Biochem immediately and see if they can transport a plasmapheresis machine to the hospital right away. I'm on my way, Mads."

After we hang up, I tell my mom the news. She slumps into a chair, releasing the tension she has been holding onto for so long. She starts to cry tears of relief. I then text Ian to let him know that a cure has been found. He tells me that he's on his way to the hospital. Mom and I stand next to my father's bed, holding his hands as we wait for Matthew and the plasmapheresis machine to show up. It feels like forever. Minutes slowly tick by. My feelings of uneasiness and panic start to rise. I keep staring at my father, waiting for that terrifying moment when he wakes up and then dies. Come on, Matthew!

"I'm here!" Matthew finally proclaims, as he pushes the machine in with him.

I sit off to the side as I watch Matthew get to work. He first has to extract my father's plasma. It is almost mesmerizing watching the machine work. His blood travels through a small tube that winds around the front of the machine and fills a compartment full of blood. The glowing blue plasma is transferred to a bottle hanging from the bottom of the machine. Once the compartment is full of plasma-free blood, the machine pumps the blood back into my dad's arm and then starts the whole process again, until the bottle is full of plasma.

"Thank you so much, Matthew!" my mom says, giving him a big hug.

"No problem, Mom. I just hope I got to Dad soon enough. Unfortunately, there are going to be more deaths. It is unlikely that we are going to be able to get to every person that is already in the late stages of this illness. I wish there was some magical way to give every person the cure right now, but there isn't," Matthew says, with a look of defeat on his face.

"Don't get down on yourself, Matthew. What you've done is incredible. I am so proud to be your sister right now," I interject. I truly am in awe of what my brother has accomplished. I have spent my whole life being jealous of his intellectual capabilities, but right now, I couldn't be happier because of them. I'm sure he will still get on my nerves from time to time, but maybe when I think about this day, I will be able to keep myself from rolling my eyes at him. Maybe.

Once the machine is done and the bottle is filled with Dad's glowing plasma, Matthew starts the process of giving my dad a bottle of my plasma. It becomes a waiting game once more. We have yet to see if this works on someone who is in the late stages of this illness.

Ian shows up after a little while and we all sit together, keeping each other company, and watching my dad to see if we notice anything happening. Late into the evening, we all decide that his veins look like they have faded a bit. We each take turns sleeping while we wait, making sure someone is alert in case my dad wakes up.

Around lunch time, Ian and I take a break from sitting and go down to the cafeteria to grab some food for everyone. I throw on the Green Bay Packer sweatshirt that Ian wore to the hospital so I can cover my arms and conceal the fact that I don't have glowing veins. I don't want to get attacked again.

＿＿＿＿＿＿＿＿＿＿＿＿＿＿＿＿＿＿

"Any changes?" I ask, once we're back.
"Nothing yet," my mom sighs.

We sit around the little table and eat our sandwiches. Not bad for hospital food. That's when we hear it.

"Marie?"

"Charles! You're awake!"

Matthew and I drop our food and rush over to my father. Ian stands and watches.

"What happened?" my dad asks weakly.

"You were in a coma. The supernova caused damage in your body, but Matthew found a way to fix it," Mom answers, stroking his hair.

"Thank you, Son."

"You're welcome, Dad. I'm so relieved that you're feeling better. Would it be okay if I take a sample of your blood to make sure you're completely healed?"

"Sure. Go ahead."

Matthew steps out of the door and finds a nurse to ask for what he needs. A moment later, the nurse wheels in a cart with the things needed for a blood draw along with a microscope and slide.

The nurse draws my dad's blood while we all stand and watch. She hands it to Matthew and leaves to continue her rounds. He puts a couple drops of blood onto the slide and looks through the microscope at it.

"It worked! Dad is healed!"

We all start cheering and hugging each other.

"I really want to stick around, but now that we know this will work, I think I should get back to the lab and assist in any way possible. We have a lot of work to do to get the cure to everyone. Keep on donating, Mads. We will need every bit of plasma we can get."

"I will."

We alert a passing nurse about what's going on. She insists that they check his vitals before allowing him to go.

"Madeline?" my father says.

I walk over to his bed, bringing Ian with me.

"Yes, Dad?"

"I don't believe I've been properly introduced to this young man."

"Dad, this is Ian. Ian, this is my dad."

They shake hands.

"It's nice to meet you, Sir" Ian says.

"I'm glad to finally meet you too. I can't say that I was too pleased with the pain you caused my daughter, though. I assume you have that all worked out?" my dad asks in his serious dad voice.

"Yes, Sir. It won't happen again. I care very much about your daughter."

"Good. I look forward to having some nice long talks with you, Ian."

Ian has a smile on his face, but he is struggling to hide the fearful look in his eyes. Nothing like having your father scare your boyfriend. I look over at my dad, and he gives me a wink.

Once the nurse is done, my father is released from the hospital. It looks like things are finally turning around and hope is being restored.

CHAPTER FORTY

VINCENT

"Give it up, Vince. You're never gonna find him," Pete says, laughing from the passenger seat of Vincent's car.

"Shut up! He's gotta be in this city somewhere," Vincent screams, desperately.

"What? You gonna knock on every door until you find him?" Pete says, sneering, making his pale corpse face even uglier.

"If that's what it takes. Now go away! I don't wanna see your face no more!" Vincent yells.

Pete disappears just as quickly as he appeared.

"He's gotta be here somewhere." Vincent says to himself, slowly slipping into madness. He hates when his friends pay him a visit. Shortly after they do, he forgets who he is and where he's going. He pulls his car over to the side of the road and unfolds the note he wrote to himself for when this happens.

1. Your name is Vincent Brown.

2. Maggie is dead.

3. The gov. killed her.

4. You're in Chicago to find the professor and his group of gov. bastards.

5. Your gonna kill them for what they did to Maggie.

Vincent looks in the backseat and sees the pile of explosives he was able to get from Pete's friend. The trunk is loaded with them too.

It's been two weeks since he made it to Chicago. Everyone he asks doesn't know who Professor McGreggor is or what Vincent's talking about. He's come close to zapping a few people with lightning out of frustration, but thinks better of it. He doesn't feel well after he uses his powers anymore, as though a poison is seeping through his veins.

He steps out of the car and continues his tedious search on foot. He walks down the sidewalk and stops when he sees someone reading a newspaper. The front headline reads:

A Cure Has Been Found!

"What does that say?" Vincent asks the portly man holding the newspaper.

"Didn't you hear? A cure has been made! Some biology student from Wisconsin was able to make a cure from his sister's plasma."

Vincent takes a few shuffling steps backwards, until his back hits a wall. His feet give out from under him and he slides to the ground. He starts breathing heavily.

"You okay there, pal?"

"What was her name? The sister." Vincent asks, in a trembling voice.

The man squints his eyes behind his wire rimmed glasses at the newspaper, searching for a name.

"Madeline. It says her name's Madeline," he answers. "Hey, you don't look so good. Would you like me to take you over to the hospital for your dose of the cure?" He points down the road at a medical clinic. Even from a distance, Vincent can see a long line of people snaking around the outside of the building, waiting for the cure.

"Leave me alone." Vincent chokes out. The man huffs, turns around, and walks away.

I never shoulda left Wisconsin. She was important all along and I left to go on this wild goose chase. Damn it!

Vincent picks himself up off the ground, muscles shaking with anger. He stumbles back to his car and climbs inside.

There's no way I'm gonna make it back to Wisconsin, now. I can't even remember my name half the time. If I'm gonna strike, I'm gonna have to do it here. Right now. They ain't gonna get me with their "cure".

He pulls the car out onto the road and drives towards the clinic. Once he's only a block away, he slams his foot down on the accelerator, picking up speed fast. He weaves around a car that's in his way and points his car directly at the building.

"I'll see you soon, Maggie!" he shouts, heading straight for the entrance of the clinic. People see him coming and jump out of the way, but it does them no good. Just as Vincent crashes through the glass entrance doors of the clinic, he shoots a bolt of lightning at the explosives in the back seat. The explosion could be heard, miles away.

EPILOGUE

Six Months Later. . .

The world is slowly getting back to a healthy normal. Once the scientists started getting batches of my paraproteins incubating in labs, it didn't take long for them to start making significant amounts of the cure. From what Matthew told me, they had hundreds of labs across the country working on it. There were a lot of people that needed it. What was left of the whole world, to be exact. It's crazy for me to think that a little part of me is going into every human being still on earth.

Biochem and other plasma centers around the world, offered to perform the plasmapheresis too. That way, more of the cure could be administered at one time.

I continued to donate my plasma for four straight months. I ended up needing to go in to the hospital for IV fluids because I started to get dehydrated and passed out a couple of times. Ian just happened to be there once when I passed out, and he insisted that I go in. I hate needles, and the thought of getting a needle poked in me every single day was almost too much, but I kept reminding myself why I was doing it. That helped me through it.

Once they had released the fact that there was a cure, people immediately started lining up outside of clinics around the world. Those that were not in their right mind, were brought by those that had already had the cure or were not too far gone from the illness. There were a few places where the police had to step in. People were fighting over who deserved to get treated first. It was a stressful time for the hospitals, having to triage so many people at once. They started with all the patients who were already in comas, but unfortunately, there were cases where the patients were too far gone for their bodies to be healed.

I saw on the news, only weeks after the word had been let out about the cure, that some guy blew up a clinic in Chicago. Why would someone do that? The poor innocent people that were waiting to get the cure died. Haven't there been enough deaths?

I finally talked Ian into going to get the cure. He kept insisting that other people needed it more than him.

"I have a confession. I'm not sure I want the cure. I'm really going to miss feeling your emotions, especially when I do this," he said, while he grabbed me and gave me a kiss so passionate that my knees almost gave out. I had those heated feelings again, stirring deep inside me. He pulled away with his eyes closed and a big smile on his face. His veins were glowing a touch brighter after that.

"You're naughty," I whispered, smiling.

Once his procedure was done, I drove him home and stayed with him until he felt completely better. He slept a lot, but I didn't mind. I am so thankful that he's going to be okay. I guess he's just going to have to work harder to know how I feel, now that he doesn't have his superpower. Looks like we are going to have to spend more time together. Can't say I am too sad about that.

There are maximum security prisons being built to hold criminals who still have their powers. They are being designed to handle any kind of powers imaginable. It's going to cost millions of dollars to build them, and I'm not sure what they are going to do with the prisons after all the people have died from the radiation poison. Although, it turns out that if these people are selective when using their powers, it is estimated that some of them may be able to survive for even a couple years before they become terminal. Matthew told me about a group of scientists working to try to manipulate his cure into a treatment that would prevent death without removing the powers, but he seemed confident that it wouldn't be possible.

It's sad to see that there are people choosing death out of pride or fear. I asked Matthew why they don't just force everyone to get the cure, but he said it comes down to freedom. If people want to choose to keep their powers, knowing they will die, that's their right. There have been so many deaths since the supernova happened. It makes me wonder if the world will ever recover from this. Over time, I'm sure everything will work out, but for right now, the population has decreased immensely.

Things are going wonderfully with Ian. As a matter of fact, we got engaged just last month. He asked me when we went for a day trip to Devil's Lake. We hiked all the way to the top of a bluff and sat on a ledge overlooking the lake. It was early spring, so leaves were just starting to grow on the trees. The sun was sparkling off the water, and I was completely mesmerized by all the beauty. But while I was looking around at the beautiful sights, Ian was looking at me. I finally realized that he wasn't taking it all in and I asked him why. He told me that I was the most beautiful sight to look at. Then he stood up, pulled the ring out of his pocket, got down on one knee, and asked me to marry him. I said yes, of course. He is the most amazing man ever. I can't wait to spend the rest of our lives together.

We told my parents the happy news that night and they were ecstatic for me. My father already knew it was going to happen. Ian is an old-fashioned kind of guy. He went to my father to ask for his blessing before proposing to me. My dad has grown quite fond of Ian. It made him proud to be able to say yes.

Matthew is receiving a Nobel Prize for his work on the cure. The ceremony takes place on December tenth in Stockholm, Sweden. It's going to be quite the occasion. We are all so proud of him. He even managed to find a girlfriend through all of this, which makes my mom even happier. She seems nice, and she's even a little nerdy, which works out perfectly for Matthew.

I have become somewhat of a celebrity here in Amherst. Everyone wants to show me their gratitude for my part in the cure. I get a lot of free meals at the restaurants here in town. And just when I think every single person in town has shaken my hand and said thank you, I get stopped by yet another person. It's hard not to get a big head, but I know that I didn't really do anything. It was all Matthew and the scientists who worked so hard to make the cure.

Today I am on my way to the hospital. Elizabeth's mom just called and told me that Elizabeth is in labor. Elizabeth had said that she wanted me to be at the hospital with her when she had her baby. I've never seen a birth, and I'm not that interested in seeing one, but I want to be there for her. I also think it will be wonderful to see the blessing of a new life being brought into this world after seeing so much death.

I head up to the third floor and ask the nurses where I can find Elizabeth. They lead me to her room down a series of hallways. I walk in on Elizabeth having a strong contraction. She's covered in sweat and breathing heavily, but she still looks so beautiful. That's how it always is with Elizabeth. She could shave her head bald and have a case of chicken pox and I'm sure she would still be gorgeous.

"Hi, Elizabeth," I say, taking her free hand. Her mom is holding the other one.

Her mom looks calm and relaxed. Things must be going well. I suppose she knows what to expect since she has done this before. I take notice of just how much Elizabeth looks like her mom. They both have dark hair, only her mom's is cut short, and they both have a petite build. Being so small made Elizabeth a very cute pregnant lady. I know it's clichéd, but it truly did look like she had swallowed a basketball.

Once her contraction is done, she gives me a weak smile, clearly exhausted.

"Thanks for being here, Madeline. I'm so scared right now."

"You're doing fine, honey," Elizabeth's mom says, wiping her brow with a cool wash cloth.

"Thanks, Mom. I just wish Philip was here."

"I know. I wish he was here for you, too. But I bet you'll see him, or at least things that will remind you of him, every day when you look at your precious baby. You will always have a part of Philip with you," her mom says.

She manages to smile and then another contraction hits. This one is a big one. I feel so bad for her, watching the pained look on her face. Once it's done, the nurse checks to see how far along she is.

"It won't be long now. You are completely dilated. When you feel the urge to push, Elizabeth, let us know."

After about five more minutes of contractions, she says she needs to push. I'm afraid she's going to break my hand, she is squeezing it so hard. She continues pushing on and off for about twenty grueling minutes. I'm in awe at how much pain the human body can tolerate.

Finally, the doctor yells, "I see the head! One more big push, Elizabeth!"

She pushes hard, her face turning a dark shade of red and the next thing I know, I hear a baby crying.

"It's a boy!" announces the nurse.

Looks like I was right about her having a boy.

"Would you like to cut the cord, Grandma?" the doctor offers Elizabeth's mom.

Elizabeth's cheeks are streaked with tears of joy and relief. After the umbilical cord is cut, they clean the baby off a bit and lay him up on Elizabeth.

"Welcome to the world, Elijah Philip," Elizabeth says, sweetly.

I lean in to look at the baby. My breath catches in my chest.

He looks just like pictures of newborn babies I have seen, with puffy eyes and a slightly coned head, but his veins are remarkably bright blue.

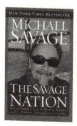    

CPSIA information can be obtained
at www.ICGtesting.com
Printed in the USA
LVOW03s0405170817
545343LV00001B/91/P